LEGAL PARTNERS

CARL U. MAXWELL

Legal Partners
By Carl U. Maxwell
Copyright © 1987, 2023
Cover art by Fotor AI
ISBN print: 978-91-89822-18-4
ISBN e-book: 978-91-89822-19-1
Published by Yabot AB, Sweden, 2023

1 – Benjamin Meyer

Moore, McKenna & Crane was one of New York City's largest and most influential law firms. In fact, an argument could be made that it was the most powerful firm in the state. Each of its eighty-seven junior partners made a million dollars each year. Each of its nine senior partners made five times that.

It sat atop the glass-walled Hudson building, taking up the top ten floors. Nine of those floors were circled by offices of the partners and senior partners, as well as the many associates and lawyers who worked on salary without a share of the profits or a say in the firm's management.

The Hudson building had been exquisitely designed so that the top twenty floors had not four corners but twelve. Twelve corner offices per floor made one hundred and twenty corner offices. That was more than enough to accommodate all the partners, with a number left over.

However, the top floor held no offices. Instead, it contained private apartments for the senior manager's entertainment facilities for the firm's clients, saunas, a small swimming pool, a small exercise room with expensive equipment, and several small bedrooms intended for the use of junior partners, who were forced to stay late in the city.

Without the top floor, there were only one hundred and eight corner offices. There were still enough for all the partners, both senior and junior. As for the twelve left over, they were available to the associates, who fought bitterly for possession.

Associate lawyers had little status and were employees, just like clerks and secretaries. They could be hired and fired at will and had no say in which accounts they worked on, their hours, or their salary. In addition, they must report to a partner and be told how to handle each case, despite their own thoughts.

Many bristled at this, but Associates did what they were told or found somewhere else to work. Since Moore, McKenna & Crane was the most prestigious firm in the city, nobody wanted to work elsewhere. All of them wanted to stay and hopefully become partners someday.

It could take more than ten years, perhaps twenty, to make a partner. Even that wasn't assured. A lawyer could work his or her entire life for the firm and not be made a partner. It all depended entirely on how they and their work were regarded by the senior partners.

Naturally, this meant that all of them were consumed with pleasing their partners to curry favor and attention. They took every opportunity to compliment partners and do favors for them.

The partners appreciated this obsequious treatment and treated the associates as serfs, there to do their bidding without question or complaint.

Of course, not all partners were equal. The chairman of the senior partner's board had the most power, followed by the eight other senior partners. The junior partners had various degrees of power, depending on their influence on the senior partners and how likely they would be elevated in the near future.

Benjamin Meyer was one of the most powerful junior partners. His acceptance to the senior partner's board was considered almost certain when Paul Irving retired next spring. Meyer was a tall, thin, hard-faced man who lived for the law and the manipulation of it.

He had fought, clawed, and worked his way up to his

present position over the past twenty years with the firm and saw no end in sight to his maneuvering and politicking. Though the infighting was fierce among associates, it paled in comparison to the politicking among junior partners, and that in itself was nothing compared to the infighting and backstabbing that took place among the senior partners.

Meyer intended to chair the senior board one day, and everything he did at the firm was aimed at advancing his position toward that goal. He was not proud of everything he had done to get where he was, but he had crushed too many men and ruined too many careers to accept anything short of his goal.

He was sitting in his large corner office, the room brightly lit by the floor-to-ceiling glass walls, gazing at the young associate standing in front of him, contemplating how she could be useful to him.

The first way she could be of use was sex, obviously. Though she stood there smiling demurely, she had made it more than clear that her body was his if he so desired. He did, in a way, but not in the same way most men would have.

Alicia Porter was twenty-eight and had worked as an associate at the firm for four years. Since she was a top graduate of Harvard Law School, her rise up the unofficial rungs of the associate's ladder had been only a little short of meteoric, a sign of a determined person and a person who knew how to fight for what she wanted and wasn't too concerned with methods.

Supposedly she was standing before his oak desk to hear his input on the case she was working on. He knew that wasn't true. She was there so he could look at her and her expensive navy blue business suit with its mini skirt that revealed just enough of her exquisite thighs to excite without bringing condemnation down on her from the more conservative partners.

Her blonde hair was perfectly brushed and combed, shoulder length, swept across her forehead from left to right, beautiful without looking like she'd spent a lot of time on it. Now, as always, even the roots were golden, though he was reasonably sure she wasn't a natural blonde.

Her jacket was open, revealing her white silk shirt beneath, and beneath that portion of the shirt visible was an outline that was clearly a brassiere, colored black, or at least a very dark shade. That, too, was meant to be seen.

She had a beautiful, slender, attractive face with a tiny, snub nose that was probably the work of plastic surgery. Her eyes were grey-blue today. Contact lenses changed them from their natural brown. Her chest pushed out firmly, leaving little doubt that she was well-built in all areas.

She stood there straight back with a respectful look as though she was eager for any drops of pearly wisdom he deigned to provide her.

She was beautiful and ruthless, and those two qualities could make her quite valuable to him in his constant battles with the other partners. And then there was her pride. One did not achieve what she had at such an early date without an incredible amount of pride in ones-self.

And that was where he found her most attractive, for he knew that for him, she would abandon all pride and dignity, grovel, beg, and do anything he wished, no matter how degrading. And power was what he truly felt lust for, power over others.

He held the power that would strip this proud, beautiful woman naked and make her beg for his attention, and that was what he found arousing and exciting. Other men might have lusted after her body, but it was the control of her mind and the domination of her will that excited Meyer.

He knew what she was after, of course. He was a rising star and could pull her along with him. That was for the long term. For the short term, she was after the corner office on the sixty-eighth floor that had recently become vacant. All the senior associates were maneuvering towards it, for it brought prestige. It was a sign of favor from on high and thus brought a share of its power to be lorded over more junior associates.

Doling out offices was too insignificant a job to interest the senior partners. It held a lot of interest to junior partners who wanted to influence those under them, and after a nasty fight, Meyer won the assignment last year. So it was he they all groveled to.

Alicia Garner was not the first of the female associates to offer him her charms in exchange for it. But, provided she performed adequately, he decided that she would be the one to get it. He could use an aide with her intelligence, beauty, and ruthlessness, provided she had nothing unpleasant like ethics or morals that would hinder her.

He motioned her around the desk, his other hand under the surface, flicking the button that locked the door. She smiled inquiringly and came around to stand beside him. Meyer looked at her with a knowing smile, then reached for her wrist.

He gripped it tightly, pulling her down to her knees as he swiveled his executive leather chair to face her. Her face showed a little surprise, but she did not fight him as he forced her to her knees before him. He held her wrist tightly, squeezing it so he knew it hurt her.

She showed a little sign of pain, though she swallowed several times and seemed tense. He sniffed, then reached out with his free hand and cupped her chin, lifting it upwards. She said nothing. He slid his hand across her cheek and under her blonde hair, stroking her neck and the side of her head.

Then he pulled her hand against his crotch, rubbing it firmly up and down against his groin. She reached for his belt, slowly undid it, then pulled his zipper down. Her soft hands reached in and worked his cock out. It was still soft, though beginning to harden as it felt her fingers around it.

He let go of her completely, sitting back in his chair and eying her with a detached expression. He had no intention of clouding his dominance of the woman with the thought that physical force was compelling her to act. No, power made her do what she was about to do, power alone. He had no need for physical strength.

She gave him a sensuous look, then, holding his cock in both her hands, she pushed her tongue far out and licked it up along the underside, slowly, firmly. She did it again, then kissed the head. He sat still, hands on the arms of his chair, watching without expression.

She slid her lips over the head and took it into her mouth, rubbing the lower part of the shaft as she slid her lips down along its length. She began sucking softly at first. Her tongue rubbed against the underside of his cockhead, stroking that most sensitive part of his organ.

It hardened within her mouth, and she slid her hands off the shaft, pushing his pants down a little to get at his balls. She cupped them in her hands, massaging carefully as her lips slid up and down his long shaft. She let it free from her sensuous lips and rubbed the saliva-coated prick all over her face, moaning softly.

It was an act, the moans, but a good one, and he gave her credit for it. She bent forward again and sucked his cock into her mouth, bobbing her head up and down rapidly, her tongue sliding against the underside. If she was nonplussed about his lack of emotion, his failure to talk, she kept that to herself.

Another point, he thought.

She stopped sucking briefly, opening her lips and closing her teeth around his cock just behind the head. She slid her mouth down slowly, the teeth scratching lightly along his shaft to give him contrast when she sucked again. She had obviously learned how to suck cock quite expertly.

She took her mouth off it and rubbed it across her face again, softly sighing. She kissed the head, then sucked, opening her lips a bit, then a bit more, sucking in the head, then, keeping the hole in her mouth small, she pressed down, and his cock forced its way into her mouth.

Yes, she was pretty good at this. He wondered if she knew how to deep throat. She would before he was done with her.

He felt his cock sparkling with tension and knew he was about to cum. No doubt she would swallow it. He didn't intend to allow her that victory. He gripped her hair suddenly, very tightly. She gasped in pain but did not attempt to pull his hand free.

He began jerking her head up and down on his cock, forcing her down far, then pulling her back up, leaving no doubt in her mind who was in control here. As he felt his cum begin, he jerked her head back, pulling her lips off his mouth and replacing them with her fingers. His hand was over hers, squeezing it down on his cock as they pumped the cock once, twice, three times, four... then he came, his sperm jetting out the tip and smacking into her forehead. She gasped and tried to pull away, but he held her hand and head in place. Wad after wad shot out and splattered against her face, dribbling down her nose and cheeks and off her lips. He gave a sigh finally, the first sound he had made, and pulled her face forward, jerking her hand off his cock. He rubbed his cock all over her face, rubbing his sperm into her pores, coating every inch from forehead to chin with his juice.

Then he flung her back. She fell on the floor and gasped in shock, staring up at him with wide eyes. He allowed himself a brief, cold smile.

"Not bad," he said. "But I've seen better." She flushed, fighting down an angry retort. He knew he'd wounded her pride by both his behavior and words, but she was saying nothing.

"Let's see what you have under those expensive clothes, Porter," he said. "Strip."

She swallowed again, eyeing him carefully, as though just then realizing how dangerous a game she was playing. Backing out now would be worse than not having come in at all. She would be finished, and she knew it. She slowly stood up, trying to hold onto whatever dignity she imagined she had left.

She removed her jacket and placed it carefully on the Chesterfield. Her hands shook slightly as they worked the zipper on her short skirt. She was undoubtedly fighting to keep from rubbing at her face, glistening with wet cum.

She slid the skirt down her long legs, giving her hips a little shimmy as she did so and stepping gracefully out of it. She threw it on the couch with her jacket, then unbuttoned her shirt. As he'd suspected, she had a black bra beneath, tiny string bikini panties, and a matching garter belt.

She stood there proudly for a moment, apparently regaining some of her conceit and pride. She slid her hands up and down her body, sliding her tongue over her lower lip as she looked at him through slit eyes again.

He almost laughed. She no doubt thought that was sexy. She still didn't realize it was the control that excited him, the power over her mind and body both.

She slid her hands up and through her hair, posing, then turned, showing him that she wore a G-string instead of panties. She turned her side to him, raising one straight leg and putting it on the couch as she reached down and slid to remove the high-heeled shoe.

She did it slowly, posing carefully, then slid down the garter and rolled down the stocking. She turned and smiled flirtatiously at him, then raised her other foot and repeated the process. She put the foot back and turned to him, undoing the garter belt and removing that as well.

He could tell that she was again confused. She hadn't expected to have to strip completely. No doubt she'd expected a quickie on the couch, perhaps with her skirt off and her blouse and bra open. But that wasn't what he waited for. He wanted her utterly, every part of her, and he wanted her to know that she was his to do with as he chose.

With only slight hesitation, she reached back and undid her lacy black bra, then removed it and put it on the couch with the rest. She gave him an inquiring look as if to ask if she needed to remove the G-string. He raised his eyebrows, and she bent forward, sliding the small scrap down her legs and stepping out of it.

She dropped them on the couch and straightened, now looking somewhat uncomfortable. She glanced at the door once, and though she tried to keep her composure, he knew she was somewhat worried about what was going on. All she'd had from him so far was silence.

He smiled inwardly, watching her squirm. He made her stand still for a full minute before he raised his hand and extended one finger, then twirled it slowly. She swallowed again, then turned around, showing him her behind.

"Spread your legs, Porter," he said.

She spread them apart about a foot.

"More, wide," he barked. She spread them wide apart. He smiled, wondering what expression was on her face now.

"Bend over and grip your ankles," he told her.

Her body stiffened and trembled slightly as if undergoing an internal fight, but then she slowly bent forward, bending far down and gripping her ankles. She looked back at him between her legs, pretending to smile. Her face, he noted, was flushed.

His eyes shifted from her face up to her ass and her crotch. Her pussy hair was brown, he noted. He sat unmoving for long seconds, then reached behind his head and scratched himself. He saw her face flush an even deeper red.

He kept her like that for another minute.

"All right," he said. "Stand up and turn around."

She did so gladly, sighing as she turned but still trying to look dignified. He would put a stop to that. He intended to use her, but he intended to break her first. He would so thoroughly humiliate her that she wouldn't think of crossing his will. Only then would he be able to trust her... to a degree.

"Sit down, Miss Porter," he offered solicitously, indicating the chair in front of his desk. Now looking confused, she padded across the thick carpet and sat uneasily in one of the chairs.

"Not going as you'd planned. Is it, my dear?" He smiled coldly. "So you want to work for me, do you, Porter?"

"Yes, sir," she said quietly.

"You'd like to share in my power, wouldn't you? You'd like me to help you into the partner's lounge, hmmmm?"

She regained her composure enough to cross her legs and give him one of those slit-eyed looks.

"What do you want, Mister Meyer?" she purred.

"For one thing, you can open your legs again."

Again, she looked surprised, and her face flushed a bit. She opened her legs again.

"Wider, put them on the arms of the chair."

She spread her legs, lifting her feet off the floor and dropping her legs across the two arms of the chair. Again, her face showed signs of discomfort and worry.

You'll have to learn to control those face blushes better, Porter, he thought. Drop a point.

"Much better," he smiled thinly.

He stared at her for a few seconds, then sat back. "Let me see you masturbate, Porter."

"What?!" At last, he'd really startled her.

"Your vocabulary does not include the word?"

"No... I... I mean, of course."

"Then do it."

"Wouldn't you rather..." She gave him a coy look. "Help me?" she completed.

"Now, as always, I will tell you what to do, and you will do it."

Now she was blushing furiously, and he could see her desperately trying to figure a way out of this. No doubt she regretted ever coming in here. One of the older partners would be so grateful to fuck her; he'd be in and out in five minutes. She probably wouldn't even have to remove her skirt.

"Let's see it, Porter. Let's see how passionate you can be with the one you love."

She seemed to think he meant himself for a moment, but then she scowled, just for a brief second, realizing he meant her, that she loved herself.

Then, defiantly, tilting her head to one side, she slid her hands onto her breasts and began to knead them. Her fingers mashed and twisted the perfect, round globes, then one hand slid down her belly and between her legs. She rubbed herself, her finger parting her cunt lips and sliding up and down the cleft.

She let her head fall backward, slumping down a little more in the chair, stroking her slit carefully as her other hand caressed her breasts. She lifted her hand to her mouth, slid a finger into it, and then sucked on it, giving him her sexy look again. Then she slid the finger against her cunt and wriggled it inside.

She pumped the finger in and out of her cunt, rubbing her clit with her thumb.

She kept looking up at him, starting to get flustered as he stared without reaction or expression. No doubt, the thought had occurred to her now that she was doing nothing but humiliating herself before him and that as soon as she was done, he would simply fire her.

He was doing his best to look bored, but it was a good thing she couldn't see his crotch, where his cock stuck out straight and hard. He wanted her to be uncomfortable. He wanted her embarrassed. He wanted her to lose her composure, her confidence.

She added a second finger to her snatch, pumping them harder and deeper, rolling her head as she moaned, sighed, and whimpered. Her ass ground down into the chair, and her crotch humped against her fingers, not energetically. That would have been too much, just a little, just enough to convince some idiot man that she was getting off.

He pulled one hand from behind his head and glanced at his watch. He saw out of the corner of his eye that she broke her carefully maintained look of bliss. He looked back at her, the same bored look on his face, and she quickly shifted her features back into those of pleasure.

She pumped more erratically with her fingers, though, and her hand squeezed her tits, mashing the flesh rather than stroking it erotically. Her skin was red, and she was breathing hard and sweating, but it had nothing to do with excitement. She was now more convinced that he was merely humiliating her, probably so he could tell everyone about it later.

She had no idea what to do, so she kept masturbating, her motions not smooth but jerky and graceless as she trembled, both with fear and embarrassment. He yawned, then looked out the window. When he turned back, she had stopped. She took her fingers out of her cunt and slowly sat up, pulling her legs off the chair arms, then standing up. She stood straight, her face angry, tight-lipped. She turned towards her clothes, and he allowed himself a smile.

He reached into his desk, pulled out a key, and tossed it onto the couch. It landed atop her skirt. She looked at it, then turned and looked at him.

”That's the key to sixty-eight-twenty-nine.”

She stared at it, then reached down and touched it as if it might fade away. She trembled visibly, then straightened and turned towards him again.

”No, I'm not going to fire you, Ms. Porter,” he smiled thinly. ”Not yet, at any rate. I may... may have some use for you.”

”Come here,” he ordered.

She stepped forward, her face still pale. He stood slowly, languorously, moving beside her. She did not meet his eyes as he looked up and down her nude body. Then he grabbed her hair suddenly, jerking her up and back. She cried in pain as he tore her hair, and her hands scrambled behind her head for his wrist.

He held her there for a few moments until she stopped struggling and lowered her arms. She was trembling again, her eyes wide, obviously frightened.

”Yes, I think someone like you could have innumerable uses,” he grinned. ”Including the obvious.”

He slid his hand onto her belly, then held her firmly by the hair. Her back arched, chest pushed out, he stroked her soft flesh, his hand sliding under her breasts, in between, then around them, before finally sliding onto the firm rounded mounds and squeezing.

He pulled his hand back, then jammed it between her spread legs, gripping her pubic mound in a steel grip, making her cry out again as pain clawed at her.

”You remember this, darling,” he said, his face but not his eyes smiling. ”You remember just who is in command, who gives the orders, and who takes them. If you cross me, I'll see that the only job left for you is fucking winos in dark alleys.”

He jerked her forward suddenly, forcing her down onto her

knees. He let go of her hair and dropped behind her, gripping her legs and jerking them wide with a sudden savage motion. He pulled out his cock and pushed it against her slit, then pushed it in.

He forced several inches of cock meat into the young blonde, gripped her hips tightly, and thrust hard. She cried out for a third time, then moaned weakly. He forced his cock into her, all the way into the balls, then began to immediately hump against her.

He held her tightly and rode her with violent movements that he knew hurt her, wanting to hurt her, enjoying the thrill of knowing she would not protest, could not protest, could do nothing but what he ordered, could only accept whatever he gave her.

His cock pounded down into her as he jerked her slender body. His hips crushed her buttocks repeatedly as he skewered her with his thick meat. He would leave bruises on her that she would remember for some time when she considered double-crossing him.

She winced and grunted and gasped from time to time but knelt there like a she-bitch being ridden by the pack leader. That was the image that sprang to his mind, and it drove him into deeper waves of lust and violence. It was not the tight sucking motion of her cunt against his prick that aroused him, but the possession and mastery of Porter.

He knew her pride. He'd seen it often in orders of her caliber, knew it and relished its destruction, reveled in riding her like a slut, like a dog, knowing how degraded she felt, down on all fours being ridden so savagely.

If she thought that she could ever again be respected by him now that he had fucked her on all fours, now that he had rutted his cock into her fuck box and watched her asshole opening and closing, she would have to be demented.

He gripped her hair again, jerking her head up and back as his hips beat a vicious tattoo against her softly rounded buttocks. He grabbed her hair and twisted her head to one side, mashing his lips against her throat. She whimpered in pain and fear.

He laughed, throwing an even more powerful series of thrusts into the blonde's cunt. His prick was spearing her with the most violent thrusts he was capable of, and still, she did not dare protest. He shoved her head away from him, gripped the back of her head, and shoved her face down against the rug, jerking her ass up with the other hand.

He laughed again, a cold, sneering laugh as his steaming jism spewed into her fuck-tunnel to slosh around in her belly like hot porridge. He grunted a few times in pleasure, then pulled out with a sigh.

He gripped her hair again, pulling her face around to his groin. She stared at him with frightened eyes, and he grinned down. He rubbed his cock through her hair, wiping off his cum, then stood and pulled his pants up. He went to a mirror in the corner and brushed his hair, not looking at her.

"That will be all, Porter," he said dismissively.

Alicia knelt there for long seconds, panting for breath, then slowly rose, her legs unstable. As if in a dream, she dressed, unable to look at him as he passed her by and returned to his desk. He began to hum as he picked up a pen and started writing, and he didn't look up as she walked out of the room, the key clutched tightly in her hand.

2 – Ellen Rogers

Matt Stuart had been setting female hearts aflutter since the day he was hired as a law clerk at Moore, McKenna & Crane. He was tall, handsome, blonde, and a scion of a wealthy and prominent family and first in his class at Cambridge. He'd made conquest after conquest among the female assistants, secretaries, clerks, and junior associates.

That was why Ellen Rogers had arranged for him to work for her. Ellen Rogers hated men like Matt Stuart and hated them with a violent passion. Of course, as a hard-core lesbian, she hated almost all men, but she hated rich, handsome womanizers the most.

Since he'd been assigned to her, she'd done her best to make his life miserable and succeeded quite well. She'd piled on work until he walked around the office like a zombie, unable to get any sleep, much less find time for romance.

Lately, she'd added a new twist, impossible assignments. She'd cleverly find duties that, on the surface, seemed easy enough but were all but impossible to complete and then tear strips off him when he failed.

She was toying with him almost, but not quite ready for a humiliating firing notice. The other night she'd given him a last-minute assignment, a chance to make up for his "ignorant blundering" of yesterday's work. Of course, it involved him staying up all night doing research, but he could hardly complain, not after he'd made a "complete and total fuckup" of his last assignment.

Today, not only would he have to turn in research that he

could not have had time to complete, but he was also due to turn in a carefully done hundred thousand-word report on an obscure segment of corporate contract law.

Yesterday, the Supreme Court overturned the entire basis of that particular segment of law. She was hoping that she'd kept Stuart so overloaded with work that he hadn't been able to look at the current legal literature and didn't even know about the pending case. She was anticipating with glee how she would tear him to shreds when his report failed to mention the supreme court's decision.

On top of his research, which she hoped would be crap, she had enough reason to fire him. She hoped he wasn't getting help from some of those sluts who'd spread their legs for him earlier. She'd come down hard on them when she'd found them helping last month and managed to find a lot of extra work to occupy their time.

So today, Matt Stuart should see his career in shreds, along with his self-respect and confidence.

Ellen didn't spend a lot of time plotting and planning, and working against Stuart. It was more or less a hobby, something done in her spare time for her amusement. Toying with and destroying those who irritated her was one of the perks she got from being a senior partner. Another was, of course, the corner office and a private apartment on the penthouse floor.

Ellen had come this far by being brilliant at her work and utterly without ethics or morals. She also knew well about men's weaknesses and used them without compunction. She had no less than three beautiful young women working for her, helping her get ahead.

Two were secretaries, both recruited by her after diligent effort. Both were paid more money by her than by the firm, for their real job was to seduce married male partners and provide Ellen with blackmail material.

The third was a lawyer, an associate, and Ellen's special little toy. This luscious, nubile, submissive young woman would do anything to obey Ellen's slightest wish. If that included fucking and sucking partners to blackmail them, then so be it.

As for those partners who were not married and who would thus be challenging to blackmail with simple sexual encounters, she arranged more complicated affairs. Her assistants would produce "little sisters," underage young girls, prostitutes pulled from the streets.

None of the men, drunk, in a sexual high, naked, could resist the "little sisters" when they joined them in bed. All of the whores were chosen for their gorgeous faces and well-developed bodies, and all were "discovered" during the act by their "big sisters," who were, of course, suitably outraged.

On discovering the ages of their bed partners, the men were all nicely chastened and cooperative.

Word of the dangers of liaisons with the three began to grow, of course, and soon nobody would touch them. That became a problem for Ellen. She had thought of this, of course, but had figured on simply firing them all and recruiting anew, but by then, they all had such damning information on her that she did not dare fire them.

Her finances had limits, and so she did not really want to recruit an endless number of little sluts, all of whom would then have to be kept on her personal payroll for an unknown amount of time. And anyway, by then, she already had control of enough partners to push her forward to the head of the ranks of the junior partners.

Getting a seat on the senior table was still a significant step, of course, and worse, there had been a major house cleaning to bring in fresh blood. Many older senior partners had retired, and young men were brought up to replace them. An opening seemed unlikely for years.

So Ellen decided to create one. Unfortunately, all the men on the senior table were careful and crafty. She hadn't been able to lure any into affairs with any of the little whores she'd placed near them. She'd hired private detectives to find out everything about their private lives, but none had been able to discover any affair that would force a resignation. Less than half were still married, having spent too much time at their jobs to keep their wives happy, and so could screw around as much as they liked. She tried tempting them with underage but no bit, so to speak. One day, she'd chosen Larry Niles simply because she heard him telling a queer joke. Also, she knew Larry's wife had died of cancer and left a teenage daughter as the only family he had left. The girl was a freshman at Harvard, and Ellen set out to use her against him.

Several young men and women were recruited to befriend and seduce the girl, into drugs, into sex, into anything criminal, whatever she could be enticed into doing. Away from home for the first time, the girl was easy meat.

Within a month, Ellen had pictures, and even a videotape of the girl in a wild sex and drugs orgy, taking cocks into every orifice, then in wild homosexual liaisons with girls, underage girls at that. Before presenting the evidence to her father, Ellen had used the girl herself. She was a pretty little blonde and so high on coke she could hardly speak. Ellen had ridden her tongue to several orgasms, wishing her father could see her as she was. Her only disappointment was that that was simply not possible.

Also not possible was seeing his face when he got the pictures and video tape, along with the note that he would resign at once or copies would be distributed throughout the office and charges of child abuse filed with the Massachusetts police.

He had complied, never knowing for sure who had been responsible. Just for the hell of it, Ellen had released the pictures anyway. Some of them, suitably censored, had even made it into the papers. The girl was expelled from Harvard and came close to being arrested.

Ellen had chortled at every new report of her father's miseries. The girl herself was beside the point. She was merely an insignificant little slut. Ellen never had a moment's guilt about what had happened to her.

The girl hadn't been able to kick her habit and eventually became a street hooker, sucking dicks for forty bucks in back alleys. Her father had a nervous breakdown and killed himself.

Ellen had forgotten both by now. Just past forty, she kept herself in vain shape. She exercised religiously and had a firm, fit, tight body. Always strong and well built, her tall, broad-shouldered, hourglass figure showed little of time's ravages.

Her face, seldom exposed to the elements, looked ten years younger than her age. Her hair was waist-long and jet-black. Her legs were endlessly long and beautifully sculpted. Her breasts sagged not at all, thanks to an expensive surgeon, and her ass was as round and thin as when she'd been a teenager.

Nobody at work saw any of this, though, not really. She wore severe, dark-colored business outfits that hid most of her figure. Her hair, she pulled straight back from her forehead and bound in a tight bun behind her head.

Stuart arrived, more like staggered into her office. His face was all puppy dog smiles, desperate for approval as he placed his long report on her desk. She looked at it idly, then up at him with a stern expression.

"The research on the Gould case?"

"Uh, I was hoping I could have a wee bit more time, Ms. Rogers, you see..."

"I'm not interested in excuses, Stuart. Get that research into me in ten minutes, or send in your resignation instead."

"Yes, Ma'am," he gulped.

"Now get out."

He bobbed his head rapidly and stumbled back out, missing her smile of satisfaction.

She picked up the report, flipping it to the summary. Her smile grew with each passing second. When Stuart brought in the research five minutes later, it was all she could do to keep her expression stern. She accepted it without comment, then opened it and smiled even harder.

There were spelling mistakes, idiotic grammar, and illogical conclusions. What was even better, he'd misquoted a few people. The thing was incomplete and shoddily put together, and Ellen rehearsed her words carefully before carrying the report and the research out to his desk.

The clerks didn't have private offices, of course. That meant everyone would get to hear his humiliation. Her voice was dripping with sarcasm but very polite; she pointed out how idiotic it was to present him with a report that was entirely out of date as of yesterday and then tore into the research.

"I think, Mr. Stuart," she concluded, "that this work is too taxing for one of your limited abilities. Stock Boy at a Seven-Eleven might be more appropriate. I suggest you apply because this firm cannot carry an incompetent like yourself any further. You may speak to Mister Hugo about your severance pay."

Everyone pretended not to watch or listen, but she knew the whole corner of the office there had heard and watched Stuart's humiliation. Stuart knew it as well, witnessed his beet-red face. She was slightly disappointed that he didn't bother to argue or offer any excuses, but then he had been awake for a long time and was probably just grateful for the chance to go home and sleep.

Next time, she'd know better.

She strode through the office, her icy eyes sending clerks and secretaries scurrying away, then took the private elevator up to the penthouse. Molly waited there. The cute little redhead had booked off sick that morning, at Ellen's instructions, and waited there for her.

Ellen always felt horny after squashing someone, and Molly, her little toy lover, would cool her off so she could get back to work later.

The girl was waiting by the front door for her, on her knees, naked. Just as Ellen had ordered. She jumped to her feet and began removing Ellen's clothing as the older woman stood there, reveling in her pleasure at Stuart's destruction.

Like almost all her lovers, Molly was short, barely over five feet tall. Ellen liked to dominate her lovers physically as well as emotionally. However, the girl was exquisitely made with luscious red curls, high firm breasts, and a tiny waist.

Her fingers were nimble as she removed Ellen's jacket and hung it up, then opened her blouse, revealing the tight black leather corset beneath. She unzipped Ellen's skirt and dropped to her knees before her mistress as Ellen raised her feet one at a time and let the girl pull the skirt out from beneath.

Clad in the leather corset, which pushed her full breasts up and together, a matching leather g-string, and garter belt, long black stockings, and high spiked heeled shoes, Ellen stood over the kneeling girl, feeling her power and relishing her destruction of another macho male pig.

"Get me a drink, whore," she said casually. She stepped past Molly as the younger woman scurried to obey. Molly was a lawyer as well, but only an associate. She had been Ellen's toy, almost a pet, for several years, doing her mistress's bidding in the office and out.

By the strictest definition, they were not lovers, for Ellen held no love for the girl. She had long ago grown bored with Molly, keeping her around more as a servant and for casual sexual use than genuine affection. Molly, of course, was utterly devoted to her and, since Ellen had broken her years ago, had no will left to speak of.

Ellen took another woman as a lover and, sometimes if the mood was on her, gifted the younger woman to friends. She used Molly to cook and clean for her, to bathe her, and to lick her to orgasms in the morning and before sleep.

She had not tasted Molly's pussy in almost four years, though now and then, she either fingered the girl to orgasms or used one of her many dildos or vibrators on her.

Molly hurried back with her drink as Ellen sat in a big overstuffed chair. The girl knelt beside her, and Ellen took the glass without comment, then slumped down into the chair and spread her legs with a sigh.

Molly quickly slid her fingers through the string of Ellen's G-string, tugging the little triangle down her legs and off. Ellen spread her legs as Molly crawled between her thighs and began stroking and licking her skin.

Ellen sipped from the glass, picked up the remote control, and turned on the TV.

Molly purred like a kitten as she slid her tongue up and down the inside of Ellen's thighs. Her fingers softly kneaded the tender flesh, then began to caress the sides of her pussy mound. Her tongue moved onto Ellen's cunt, teasingly sliding up and down on either side of her cleft, her fingers following, rubbing gently.

Ellen spread her legs more, then brought her feet up onto the edge of the armchair. She slid her hand onto Molly's head, sliding her fingers through the girl's soft curls, petting her much as she would a cat or dog.

Molly's fingers began to work up and down against Ellen's slit, massaging slowly, gently, sliding down between the puffy cunt lips and sawing along between them. She pressed her tongue against the slit and ran it up and down, moistening it as her fingers pried the wet pink flesh apart.

She held Ellen's twat open, so her tongue could rasp across her pink cunt meat. She pressed the tip of her tongue into the hole and twisted it from side to side as she probed deeper inside Ellen's crotch, sliding it in as far as she could get it until her lips and face were mashed up into Ellen's cunt meat.

She wiggled her tongue up and down inside Ellen's cunt tunnel, her lips sucking over and over like a vampire sucking blood. Her nose pressed against Ellen's clitty, rubbing steadily, grinding up and down against the tender little fuck button.

Ellen sighed with pleasure, leaning back in the chair and sipping her drink. Plots and plans slid through her mind as she contemplated how best to stave off challengers at work and how to bring down competitors on the senior table.

Molly's sucking and tonguing soon drew her mind away

from work. She thought briefly about her girlfriend and current lover, Charlotte, a stockbroker with a very long tongue, wondering whether she should invite the blonde for dinner that evening. Alex would appreciate hearing about what she'd done to the Stuart punk.

Then her mind swirled away from any real reflections to float on a blissful pool of sensuous delight. Her hand trembled, and she put the glass down, groaning in delight, bringing both hands down onto Molly's head.

She let her head fall back, rolling it slowly from side to side as she luxuriated in Molly's experienced tongue work. Every time the girl's nose ground over her clitty, she felt a little fire buzz in her loins.

Molly gently dug the twin lips wider, then slid her tongue out of Ellen's fuck tube and began to work directly on her clitty. Her tongue rasped over the little nubbin, soft and slow, building up the pressure inside Ellen's groin, easing her higher and higher into the realm of sexual pleasure.

She began to lick harder, still using the same slow, steady pacing. She probed at her hole with her middle finger, then screwed it up into Ellen's cunt to the knuckle. She twisted it from side to side, rolling her knuckles against Ellen's cunt lips as her tongue became more active.

Ellen began moaning, her ass grinding into the chair seat as she drew her legs back against her body and arched her back. Her body shuddered as an orgasm washed through her. Her eyes closed tightly, and her stiff nipples pointed towards the ceiling as she jerked Molly's face hard into her crotch.

She sighed and let her legs slowly fall back to the floor, easing up on Molly's head. She lifted the glass from the table beside her, sipping from it, letting the cool liquid slide down her dry throat.

Molly resumed her slow, steady lapping against her cunt meat, her finger sliding in and out of Ellen's cunt tunnel. She pulled the finger free, then slid it into her mouth, sucking on it as she looked up at Ellen's face.

She slid her lips against Ellen's cunt opening and shot her tongue up into the older woman's fuck pipe, scooping out bubbling hot cunt milk. She drank it down, then slid her tongue back onto Ellen's fuck button as she slid two fingers into the tight sheath.

She began opening and closing her fingers, prying at the elastic walls of Ellen's fuck tube, stretching the tube repeatedly, licking at the fuck honey that drooled out of the hole.

Her lips slid against Ellen's clit, and she sucked deeply, drawing the little bud in between, then humming to set her lips vibrating. She pumped her fingers in and out of Ellen's fuck tube, grinding them against her clitty on each stroke.

Ellen was becoming much more aroused than she'd thought she would. She had planned on a simple tongue job or two and then back to work. Her guts were cramping and boiling, her mind tumbling with lust as she mashed Molly's face against her crotch.

She tightened her fingers in Molly's hair, pulling her into the chair. She gripped her hair in both hands as she drew the tiny woman up against her. Their lips melded, their tongues dancing together. Ellen's lips sucked and chewed hungrily on Molly's as she pulled the girl's head from side to side.

The two wriggled around until they faced each other sideways on the big chair. Molly slumped down, her back bowed across the plush arm, her legs spread. Ellen knelt between her legs, her hands stroking her thighs. She slid her right leg through Molly's, gripping the younger woman's leg and drawing it across her chest.

Their cunt mounds pressed tightly together, both hot and dripping. Molly groaned as Ellen mashed her cunny down against her. Molly humped upwards, the motion crushing her fuck pad into Ellen's, rasping the tender meaty mounds against each other.

Ellen gripped her leg tighter, yanking it upwards, using it as leverage to grind her pussy back at Molly. Molly curled her leg around the older woman, drawing her into her body.

Ellen's hands slid down onto the young redhead's fat tit mounds, already hot and swollen as they pressed against her tight, straining skin. Her fingers stroked lightly for a moment, then clamped down tightly, squeezing and kneading the sensitive flesh as she repeatedly mashed her fingers into the malleable meat.

She slid a hand into Molly's hair again, jerking her head upwards as she brought her face down. Their lips met in a crushing embrace, their tongues sliding through and into each other's mouths in a wet, slurping, sucking tongue duel.

Their crotches ground together in a slow rhythm, rapidly building in speed and pressure. Their breathing was harsh and ragged, their hands roving quickly, squeezing, fondling, and groping each other everywhere.

Ellen came, grinding furiously, her hips undulating with bliss as she mashed her hot pussy onto Molly's. She arched her back, her fingers around Molly's titties, clawing at her tender mounds as she grunted repeatedly.

Then she fell forward, collapsing onto the petite woman as she panted for breath. Molly showered her throat and cheeks with kisses, whimpering with her unsatisfied need. After a few long seconds, Ellen rose and slid back against the other arm of the chair.

"Go get mister big," she said.

Molly gasped with delight and leaped out of the chair, running across the room to a cabinet, then running back with an enormous rubber cock. She slid into place against the other chair, practically lying on the seat of the big chair, her head and shoulders propped against the arm, her legs bent, spread wide, and drawn back against her chest.

Ellen stared down at the girl's slimy-wet fuck entrance, licking her lips hungrily as she slid a hand onto her fuck mound and rubbed it up and down. She held the fat double-headed dildo in her other hand, having taken it from Molly. It was a good twenty inches long and thicker than almost any cock.

She rubbed one of the heads up and down the redhead's cunt slit, rubbing harder and pressing it deeper with each passing second. She probed at the girl's cunt tube, then thrust forward, forcing the rounded head in through her tight cunt lips.

She twisted it in slow circles, then slid it out again. The red-furred cunt lips popped closed on emptiness, but only for a minute. She again rubbed the rubber cockhead up and down the slit, then penetrated the mewling redhead again, sliding the head into her snatch and twisting it in circles.

She drew it back again, then again popped it in. She drew it back just a tiny bit, as though she were going to pull it free again, but then she thrust deep, the cockhead stabbing a good six inches into the redhead's quivering fuck tunnel, drawing the slightly thinner shaft behind. Molly gasped and then shuddered, cumming furiously. Her legs bounced and jerked in mid-air, and her hands squeezed her fat titties repeatedly as she let out a series of small grunts.

Ellen fucked the dildo in and out in furious motions, rasping it hard against the girl's clitty as she came. She pressed down against the top of her fuck-button, grinding it down against the pistoning dildo as Molly shuddered and jerked and trembled through her orgasm.

Only when it had subsided did Ellen resume the careful inward motion of the dildo. She had fucked the rubber cock up and down inside Molly but used only the first six inches. Now she slowly pushed it deeper, driving the head into the base of her fuck tunnel, grinding it against the redhead's cervix deep inside her box.

She twisted it from side to side, then pumped it slowly. Molly groaned, her eyes fluttering as Ellen fucked her with the bloated rubber cock. Weak from her orgasm, all she could do was stare through blinking eyes as her mistress used more than half the dildo to skewer her tight fuck sheath.

Ellen buried it deep, then moved herself forward. She slid the other end against fuck box, sighing in pleasure as her cunt lips were pried open and slid over the round head. She eased her crotch closer to Molly's, sliding more rubber cock into her belly.

She shivered with delight at the feel of the rubber as it glided over her pussy lips, rasped over her clitty, and moved into her elastic cunt pipe. She took it deep until she could press her cunt lips firmly against Molly's.

The two women ground their pussies together, each movement jarring and twisting the thick dildo within them.

Their bodies were nailed together by the long fuck spike within them, and their every move produced moans of pleasure.

Ellen began to hump up and down, her cunt sliding up and down the length of the dildo. Her movements drew some of the rubber sword out from Molly's depths, the long rubber fuck tool moving jerkily inside the two of them.

Little Molly yelped and gasped several times as the hard rubber nose of the fuck pole mashed against her cervix, yet she did not restrain its jerking and pumping. Instead, she reached across and caressed Ellen's breasts with both hands, her fingers finding the hard stiff little nipples and pinching them, then rolling them from side to side.

They kissed again, their tongues slithering like snakes, first in Ellen's mouth, then Molly's, then Ellen's.

Ellen rolled the girl onto her front, her entire upper torso dangling over the arm of the chair as Ellen gazed down at her round buttocks and tight little gash. She knelt behind her, gripping the base of the dildo where it protruded from her body, then began to fuck Molly.

She humped down into the smaller girl's tight pussy with almost twelve inches of rubber cock, producing gasps and whines, and whimpering moans from the dazed younger woman. She fucked the cock into her with greater and greater power, her eyes crazed with lust as she watched it pump in and out between Molly's cunt lips.

Her hands squeezed Molly's small round ass cheeks, slapping them several times, her hands cracking down to squeeze the soft flesh, her nails digging into the tender meat-like claws. She rutted into the mewling redhead with savage strokes, her hips slapping against the rapidly reddening buttocks.

"You like cocks, don't you. Dirty little whore. Dirty slut girl," she hissed, gripping Molly's hair in one hand and jerking it up hard, forcing the slighter woman's upper body high so she could squeeze her titties with her other hand.

She let her drop, her hands gripping Molly's thighs instead, forcing them wider as she pounded the dildo down into her fuck pipe. She let go of the dildo every few seconds, continuing her humping motions. The dildo pumped inside their cunts, rasping across their clitties and twisting inside their bellies.

Molly began to cum, crying out in pleasure as her cunt spasmed and shook. Ellen climbed off, gripping it in her right hand. She started pounding it down into the trembling, writhing redhead's gash with deliberate force and speed, reaming out her cunt pipe with cruel power.

Molly didn't care about the pain. All she cared about was the blinding waves of sexual bliss that were tearing across her mind. She could hardly think, see, or hear. All she could do was feel, feel her body shaking, feel her insides quivering and rolling, feel the hard, thick cock tool as it pistoned inside her abdomen.

Ellen gripped her hair, jerking her back onto the chair, turning her over onto her back even as she continued to pound the dildo into her fuck sheath. She let her head hang over the arm of the chair, then squatted above it, lowering her pussy onto the redhead's dazed face. Molly's tongue began to push out against her instinctively, but Ellen was already in a state of powerful, heightened sexual pleasure. She needed no flittering tongue, not even flicking fingers. She jammed her cunt down onto Molly's face, putting almost all her weight on it as she ground her pussy against the girl's flesh.

She humped back and forth, her cunt meat rubbing against

Molly's nose and cheeks and lips and forehead and jaw. She coated the redhead's grimacing, bleary face with her cunt milk even before she cursed in pleasure and came.

She gripped the back of Molly's head and rode it like it was a horse, humping and grinding and bouncing over it as she drooled more fuck honey down over Molly. Molly's tongue slid across the dripping cunt entrance more by accident than anything else as Ellen humped desperately and quivered with delight.

3 – The Accountant

John watched as the girl bent over further, opening the lower drawer of the filing cabinet. She was wearing loose pants, but they were white, and as she bent, they tightened over her buttocks, showing the dark outline of the string bikini underwear she had on beneath. He stepped forward, walking past her. Just as he passed, his hand shot in between her thighs and gave her crotch a hard squeeze.

She yelped in shock, jerking forward and half falling into the file drawer. He snickered and grinned at her as she turned and glared back. He tauntingly slid his tongue over his lip as he walked down the hall. Served her right for having an ass like that.

He gave a peremptory knock on a door, then opened it and went through, pushing it closed behind him.

"What do you want?" Alicia glared.

"Is that any way to greet a colleague?" he grinned, leaning over her desk.

"Don't you have any work to do? Surely there must be a few secretaries or legal clerks to feel up."

"So much work, so little time," he sighed. "Speaking of which, you were in dear old Meyer's place for a while there, with the door locked, I might add. Going over anything in particular?"

"None of your business."

"When you finally came out, you went straight to the lady's room, where you spent another goodly time."

"Don't you have anything to do but spy on me?" she glared.

"Not really, no. I take it Meyer is giving you the corner office?"

"As it happens, yes."

"You must have given him some ride. Nancy Jenkins and Holly Oaks both fucked him yesterday for that office."

"I don't know what you're talking about," she sniffed.

"Uh, huh. So tell me, how big is he down there? He's kind of skinny everywhere else."

"Fuck off, John."

"Oh, come on, Alicia, old girl. I just wanted to know if I could help you."

"Help me with what?" She stared suspiciously.

"In anything your dear little heart desires."

"And why this sudden offer?"

"It's obvious you're going to make partner long before I will, tit for tat, one hand rubs the other and all that stuff. I could come in quite useful. After all, what with your new... duties, you may need someone to cover the actual legal work from time."

"You're a real slime, John."

"Yes, so?"

"I'll think about it. I may have other... help in mind."

"Well, if it's that cute little blonde boy you've had your eyes on, the one old ice crotch stole as her assistant, you can forget it. She fired him."

"What? Stuart?"

"Uh, huh. Humiliated him right in front of everyone, just like always. That's about the tenth clerk she's destroyed in the last couple of years."

"Stinking bitch. I bet she didn't even fuck him either."

"Oh, my sweet little dear, surely you jest."

”Huh?”

Let's say that you could have used the same tactics on her as you did on Meyer.

”You mean she's queer?”

”As a thirty dollar bill.”

”You think every woman who won't fuck you is queer.”

”No. I think every woman who won't fuck me is either queer or dumb, except, of course, your lovely self. But as for old comb hair, she's been carrying on with a little redhead from the sixtieth floor for several years. In fact, both of them are currently missing, so I guess they're up in the spider woman's lair celebrating her latest kill.”

”What's the redhead's name?”

”Molly O'Hara.”

”Don't know her. Oh, wait, real short, with long hair?”

”That's her.”

”I've seen her around. Cute thing.”

”I certainly think so, but so far, nothing,” he sighed.

”If she's a queer, you can forget it. And if she belongs to Rogers, you're taking your life in your hands. I don't know why she hasn't gotten around to destroying you already.”

”I'm beneath her notice and not in the way.”

”If she's queer,” Alicia pondered, ”and we could prove that she would be knocked out from the senior table. Moore hates fags.”

”Well, why don't you drape yourself across her lap while I get a camera?”

”Fuck you, John. No, I don't intend to get fired myself, but maybe we could catch her and the redhead together.”

”It's been tried. They're both far too careful.”

”Then we need a Trojan whore,” Alicia grinned. ”Some

little slut that will cooperate and lure the spider woman out where we can spray her with bug juice."

"And how do you propose getting some sweet young thing to do that?"

"Why that's your job, John," she grinned. "You're supposed to be such a cocksman; surely you can seduce some starry-eyed secretary and get her to play along."

"I'm supposed to convince some cute little thing to turn over to women?"

"Shouldn't be hard," Alicia sneered.

"And convince her to do so with the spider woman and let us tape it? That's not very likely, now, is it?"

"How you do it is your problem. Find some secretary and buy her off. It shouldn't take much. What do those sluts make in a month anyway? A lousy couple of grand?"

"She'd need another job elsewhere."

"I think I can arrange that."

"Hmmmm, well, I'll see what I can do. Think your new squeeze will cooperate?"

"Why don't we see if we can do things without him. Then I can surprise him."

"Just don't forget to give credit where credit is due."

"Of course, John. Would I take credit for your idea?" She looked guilelessly at him, but he was not fooled. His eyes narrowed, and he thought about ways to ensure her future help. A tape of her and Meyer might come in handy.

He went down the hall to the elevators, then took one upstairs to sixty-six. There he went to Jack Rowan's office and gave the secretary a hot and wet kiss.

"John," she sighed, "You'll get me in trouble."

"Won't I, though," he grinned.

"What are you doing here? Mister Rowan is in his office, and you know he doesn't like you."

"Won't be long, dear. I want to borrow the latest batch of resumes you've gotten in."

"Whatever for? You don't rate an assistant, John."

"Doing a favor for a friend, darling." He slid his hand down onto her breast and squeezed.

"John!" She pushed his hand away and turned to check Rowan's closed door. She gave him a frown, then went over to the filing cabinet and pulled out a thick file of resumes, the ones that had arrived in the last month.

"Thank you, my sweet lady, of the golden thighs," he grinned, giving her ass a squeeze as he took the file from her.

"You're such a pig," she smiled.

He took the file to the library and quickly sorted through it. First, he eliminated all the male applicants, which was ninety percent of them. He grabbed the most recent college yearbooks from the most prominent law schools, and dropped them onto the desk, then began sorting the girl's resumes, putting those from the same schools together.

He had the shell of a plan, but it would require someone new and no cheap secretary. He didn't see the dragon woman screwing around with a cheap little tart she couldn't trust. No, she would need a new law clerk, and John would find her one.

He began looking up each girl in the yearbooks, searching for the real beauties, ranking each according to the small head and shoulders shot in the book. He thought there were three or four that really stood out: real dolls. With Meyer's help, one of them would become Ellen Roger's next law clerk assistant.

He picked up the phone and called research.

"That you, Chang? It's John. Listen. I want you to check

out several people for me; they're all law students. I need pictures of each from several angles, not in heavy coats. If you could get them in bikinis, it'd be nice."

He listened for a few moments, then made a face.

"You're a real smart ass, Chang. This is for someone higher up. He's looking for a friend, so to speak. I'll ship you the names, and you get someone to their schools and check 'em' out."

* * *

Miranda Bonner had, at one time, been pleased with her looks. After all, when she was little, adults used to smile at her and pat her head and cheeks, and when she grew into a teenager, boys would come running at a glance.

After entering law school, she discovered that beauty had its drawbacks. She was regarded by many other professors, and even many of the male students, as being an intruder. Nobody took her seriously. The professors seldom called on her, and she was the victim of numerous subtle and not-so-subtle attempts at seduction from her teachers.

On the advice of her Aunt, a lawyer out in Texas, she had treated them all politely but declined. On two occasions, she had been forced to accept grades that were certainly less than deserved, and on one occasion, had had to drop a class entirely because of the teacher's sexual demands.

It wasn't that she was a virgin, but she didn't intend to fuck teachers to get the grades she deserved. She worked hard for those grades and refused to demean herself by fucking dirty old men. It infuriated her that she could do nothing about their harassment, but Aunt Rita clearly knew those who rocked the boat would be tossed over the side.

She had also warned her that even after graduation, she would have to endure continued harassment at whatever firm hired her. Too many creepy jerks in the legal world thought they were God's gift to women.

Finding a tactful way of dealing with them and putting up with the crap assignments a woman was given when she refused to literally kiss their asses was something she'd have to master if she hoped to make it in this business. So she swallowed her pride and anger and accepted the lowered grades, not reporting the squeezes, the pats, the gropings, and dirty suggestions.

She was tempted to at least threaten to complain, but as a poor scholarship student, she could not afford to make enemies. The university could yank her scholarship, and then where would she be? She'd been fortunate to get in, in the first place. She'd never get another.

She continued her studies, waiting for first-year finals and replies to the resumes and applications she'd sent across the state. She was so busy with her studies and hectic life that she never noticed the odd little oriental man who showed up here and there and snapped her picture.

* * *

"Oooooh, aren't you adorable?" John sighed as he gazed down at the glossy eight-by-tens in front of him. The girl was blonde, her hair straight but thick and full, falling around her shoulders in golden waves. Unlike Alicia's, he thought this one's looked real. She had an adorable little girl face, with big blue eyes and a tiny snub nose. Her lips were full, though her mouth was small, and she had a fantastic body.

One of the pictures was obviously taken through a window.

The girl was removing her shirt. Beneath it was a tank top. The picture had been snapped as the girl drew her arms back and her breasts pushed out firmly against the tank top. Another photo showed her jogging in a pair of shorts and a sweatshirt. A third had her walking casually along a sidewalk, wearing jeans and a blue shirt.

Several others were taken in the campus swimming pool. The girl, Miranda was her name, wasn't wearing a bikini, but the rather conservative one-piece suit still revealed her figure quite nicely, and quite a nice figure it was.

The girl was short, which was what he was aiming for. Rogers seemed to prefer short women if the redhead and that little secretary he'd seen up on the penthouse floor were any indication. She was adorably cute, in a fresh, innocent way, but had a dynamite body, a narrow waist, a round ass, and high, large but not too large breasts.

Her marks were good but could have been better, and she was on a scholarship. That made her vulnerable as hell, especially if she wasn't rich. He checked her file and found that her father was a fireman and her mother a secretary. Excellent! She was a little nobody from a nothing family. If he worked it right, she'd have to be his little Trojan whore.

He'd have to be careful, though. Girls like her, like Alicia, could use those hot little slits between their legs to worm their way into somebody's affections and turn the tables. He'd grab her fast, use her for his scheme, and then make sure she was gone.

And maybe if he worked things right, he'd get to fuck her before she went, her and that little bitch Alicia.

* * *

Alicia clenched her teeth as Meyer slid his hand up under her skirt. He was doing that all the time now, not just copping a quick grope like John did but fondling her openly, intimately, possessively as if he had every right to touch her wherever and whenever he wished.

Today she wore a long skirt, but as she stood beside his desk, he quite calmly rubbed her pussy, his hand under her skirt, inside her panties, fingers probing at her slit as she tried to explain the case sitting open on the desk.

It was his casualness that was unnerving. He displayed no lust or excitement. He was, in fact, gazing at the case file in a steady, contemplative fashion, listening politely as she explained the details, acting as normal as could be, as if he didn't have his hand up her skirt and his fingers inside her gash.

He grabbed her arm suddenly and pulled her down across his knees, lifting her skirt high over her head. He shifted her weight forward so her ass stuck into the air, then slid his hand onto her cunt mound, squeezing it. He still said nothing in the way of intimate conversation, silent as he caressed her round buttocks.

He pulled her panties down and off, then resumed carefully exploring her crotch and ass. His fingers pried at her snatch, spreading her cunt lips, though not entering. A finger probed at her rectum but again dipped lightly.

She cursed silently, glaring impotently at the fabric that covered her head, wishing again that she had chosen someone more manageable than Meyer, someone more... normal as well. He was such a cold, arrogant bastard that half the time, he scared her, and the other half infuriated her.

She lay across his lap for long minutes. His hands stroked

her backside, now and then sliding in between her thighs and rubbing her pussy. Sometimes his hands lay on her ass, not moving. She had a sudden vision of him reading the case file, rubbing her ass casually, almost like he was petting a cat in his lap.

Or a pussy, she thought.

His phone buzzed, and he said hello.

"Send him in," he said. Alicia's eyes widened, and she tried to pull herself up. He slapped her ass sharply and pushed down on her back. She heard the door open and a man's voice.

"Ready for lunch, Ben?"

"Hello, Austin, yes, just about."

"I see you've got an important case you're working on," the man's voice said with an amused tone.

"This? It is rather attractive, don't you think?"

"Very! Who is it?"

"She'd rather remain anonymous just at present. Want a feel?"

"I don't think my wife would approve."

"I don't suppose mine would either, but a man can hardly resist an ass like this."

"One of the secretaries?"

"Hmmm? No, one of the lawyers, actually. Stop squirming, girl," he said, slapping Alicia's ass again.

"You've got her well trained. I see."

"She knows what she wants and will do whatever it takes to get it. Spread your legs for my friend, darling, and let him see your assets."

Alicia was frozen in place, mortified at being seen like this and fearful that he would pull back her skirt so the man, whoever he was, would see her face. She couldn't bear to face him. It would be too humiliating.

"Spread those pretty legs, darling, or you'll have to leave the room," he warned.

Alicia jerked her legs wider apart, trembling weakly, her skin becoming cold and clammy. She recognized the voice now, Austin Reed from Farrow & Reed, the firm's accountants.

"Ahh, my, it must be nice to have power," Reed sighed.

"It has its ups and downs," Meyer said wryly. Reed laughed.

Meyer continued to stroke her buttocks as he talked. Alicia closed her eyes, even though she could see nothing through her skirt. She prayed Reed would leave and Meyer wouldn't expose her. Her identity, that is.

"I'll see you downstairs, Austin. I have to take care of a bit of business here first. You could help if you like. I'm sure the little lady wouldn't object if you used the facilities."

"It's tempting, Ben, but..."

"Oh, come on, man. How often do you get offered an opportunity like this?"

Meyer put both arms under her belly and stood up, lifting her without effort. He set her down on his desk, her ass sticking out over the edge and her skirt still wrapped around her head.

"Go ahead, Austin, take a shot at it."

"She won't mind?"

"Hell no, the little slut would fuck a doorknob if she could. Her pussy's too tight, though."

Alicia felt hands on her buttocks and knew at once they weren't Meyer. She was in a desperate quandary. She couldn't stop Reed without jerking her skirt down, and she just couldn't do that. Besides, she wasn't sure Meyer wouldn't order her to lay back on the desk. What would she do then? She couldn't defy him.

She felt cheap and dirty and almost sick as she felt Reed's hand slip between her thighs and squeeze her pussy.

"Wish my secretary would do this," he sighed.

"They'll all do it, Austin, if the price is right."

"What's this one charge?" Reed enquired. She heard the sound of a zipper and then felt a hot, thick cock pressing against her vaginal opening.

"Right now, just a corner office."

Alicia let out a grunt of pain as Reed's hard cock was thrust into her box. He was neither expert nor gentle. His enthusiasm for the sweetly rounded backside and the small fuck mound between her soft thighs made him ram his cock deep inside her and keep pushing until his balls were pressed against her.

"Ahhhhh," he sighed.

"Tight, isn't she?" Alicia heard Meyer say.

"Very nice in there," Reed replied.

He mashed his hips into her buttocks, his hands gripping her hips. He ground himself in a slow, circular motion, twisting his cock inside her silky fuck pipe. Then he drew back, his cock sliding down the length of her pipe. It halted briefly, then thrust back into her. His hips mashed her thighs against the edge of the desk painfully, and she gasped.

"She loves it," Meyer laughed.

Alicia felt her dress pull higher, hands tugging it over her belly and then under her arms. She gulped nervously, her skin hot with anger and humiliation. Her bra was unclipped, and hands, she didn't know whose, but thought they were probably Reed's, began fondling her fleshy mammaries from the sides.

Reed's cock began to pump inside her, fucking with

hurried, eager strokes, his hips slapping against her buttocks and knocking her thighs into the desk. His hands slid beneath her chest and fingered her nipples, then pinched them tightly.

She burned with rage, her mind filled with images of violent carnage and devious, horrible revenge. She vowed to punish Meyer someday, and Reed too, the pig. Unfortunately, she would have to continue supporting Meyer to get him a senior partnership. That angered her almost as much as the two men using her like a beast, a mindless piece of meat.

The thought that she had gone through so many late nights of cramming sweated through all those tests, including the bar exam, only to be fucked like a dog across some bastard's desk, like some two-bit whore, enraged her. Yet there was nothing she could do but take it.

Reed was fucking harder now, panting and groaning in pleasure as his prick pistoned inside her cunt tube. She could feel his excitement through his throbbing prick each time he halted his movements briefly to grind his crotch into her buttocks.

Then he gave a final furious series of thrusts and jammed his pole into her with a groan of exultation. She could feel his sperm pumping into her, knowing his seed was spewed into her belly, drooling down into the deep center of her womb.

"If you ever decide you don't want her, Jon, just let me know," he sighed.

"You don't even know what she looks like," Meyer grinned.

"Who cares what she looks like? I can always put a bag over her head."

The two men laughed, and Reed's cock slid back down her fuck tunnel and out. There was a brief wait, then another cock probed at the entrance to her sheath. It thrust into her with the same speed as Reed's, quickly filling her pussy with its bulk.

It occurred to Alicia that she didn't know whose cock it was, though she assumed it was Meyer. They could be playing a game with her, and for all she knew, there were a dozen of them there. Again there was nothing she could do. She was as much Meyer's belonging now as if she were a hooker and he her pimp.

His cock began to drive back and forth inside her cunt, his hands resting casually on her buttocks.

"So, how was your golf game yesterday? Meyer asked.

"Not bad, though I was one over."

"How about Frank?"

"Two under, the bastard. When are you going to be free for a game?"

"Don't know. I've got a big workload here."

His cock continued pumping steadily inside her tunnel. It was almost as though he were ignoring her and simply sharpening a pencil or straightening his tie. Alicia felt he must be acting like that on purpose. He was deliberately insulting her.

She wondered if it was a game to him. Maybe he didn't need or want her help at all. Perhaps he was just insulting and degrading her for sport and would tire of her and get rid of her in a few days after he'd had his friends fuck her and humiliate her.

She was out of her depth with him. All the other men who had fucked her had been so overwhelmed with happiness and gratitude that they were putty in her hands. Yet Meyer fucked her as casually as he blew his nose. It was amazing, eerie, and a little scary.

It was also tremendously demeaning and mortifying. She wished she'd never met the pig, had never come to work for this rotten company, or had never become a lawyer. She was miserable, clutching the skirt around her head as Meyer's prick rutted into her pussy, hoping he would finish soon and leave.

"Why don't you go get the car, Austin? I'll be down in a minute."

"Okay. Don't get carried away now," Reed laughed. The door opened and closed, and Alicia felt her skirt jerked up and completely off her. Meyer gripped her hair and lifted her upper body off the desk, pulling her back against him.

He slipped his cock out of her snatch and pushed her down to her knees in front of him, then pointed his cock at her face as he pumped it in his fist. Alicia just had time to close her eyes before his juice spits onto her face.

Wads of cum spurted against her cheeks and nose, and then Meyer rubbed his cock all over her skin, spreading the juice around.

"More face cream for you, Porter," he said, his voice amused. She opened her eyes and glared up angrily.

"You bastard!" she hissed.

"I sure am, baby. That thought just occurred to you?"

"I didn't agree to fuck all your shitty friends for that office!"

"What you agreed to, Porter, explicitly or implicitly, was to do whatever I told you to in exchange for my influence helping you into a partnership. The office was just a down payment."

She continued to scowl, and he smiled cruelly.

"You'll fuck whoever I tell you to, Porter. You offered your cunt for my use, remember? So it's up to me to use it as I wish."

And she had to admit, he had her over a barrel. And with any luck, that might be her next sexual position.

4 – Miranda Bonner

Miranda sat straight on the soft leather couch, her hands in her lap, her legs tightly closed. She was eyeing John Bauer Sr. warily, her mind beginning to weigh dangers and options.

She was wearing a navy blue jacket over a white silk blouse. A long white ruffled skirt hung just above her knees, and she wore a pair of business-like white pumps. Her blonde hair was carefully pinned back behind her head.

She was attired in as conservative and business-like manner as possible, the effect calculated to override anyone's perception of her as a blonde bimbo with big tits. Clearly, the effect was not working on John Bauer Sr., whose eyes showed him to be a sleazy, calculating bastard of the worst sort.

He'd used every opportunity so far to make physical contact with her. Oh, nothing clearly across the line. He hadn't grabbed her ass, for example. Instead, he brushed her hair, gripped her shoulders several times, patted her arm, gripped her hand too long, and pressed his thigh against hers as he sat alongside her on the couch in his office.

She'd been astounded to get a positive reply from this firm. She and her friend, Susan, had sent them resumes more as a joke than anything else. Everyone knew only the top students in the best schools had any hope of getting in here. She was not among the best, and neither was her school.

A summer clerk job here would do wonders for her career prospects. If she could get in here, she was almost guaranteed to become a millionaire someday. She hadn't slept in days, the anticipation and anxiety making her stomach sick as she tried to imagine every possibility, including that the letter had been sent by accident.

She'd also been prepared for an interview by a patronizing, sexist pig. She had not, however, been prepared for something as bad as John Bauer Sr. If his hands had been bad, his language was worse. It was leering, lecherous, patronizing, and filled with innuendo and double entendres.

His hand slid up, and he felt the earring dangling from her right ear.

"This is very nice," he said.

"Thank you, sir," she replied nervously.

His fingers touched her ear lobe as she swallowed with growing nervousness.

"Tell me, Miranda, would you like this job?"

"Of course, Mister Bauer."

I am in a position to offer it to you. The decision is entirely up to me. One of the senior partners, Ms. Rogers, is looking for a law clerk for the summer, and you fit the bill nicely. Would it bother you to work for a woman?"

"Of course not." She'd love to work for a woman and not worry about creeps like Bauer.

His hand trailed down her cheek and under her throat. She turned her head away, blinking rapidly as her skin flushed. He grinned, his eyes sliding up and down her body.

"Of course, we set a very high standard here, you know. We expect a lot out of our clerks."

"I...I realize that, sir," she gulped. His hand slid down onto her knee, and his fingers seized the hem of her skirt, rubbing the fabric between them.

"This is nice material? Silk?"

"No, sir. I don't think so."

"It's very nice, whatever it is." His hand slid the hem upwards a couple of inches, then let it go.

"You're quite an attractive girl, Miranda."

"Thank you, Mister Bauer."

"Image is almost as important to us as reality, you know. It helps when the clients see so many young, attractive people around. But you should let your hair down. I'm sure it would look better."

"I do at school, sir, but I thought..."

"To make a more conservative image? Oh, that's not necessary. We aren't all that conservative here. Let it down for me. I'd like to see how it looks."

You need this job, she said to herself. She pulled the clips from her hair, letting it fall around her shoulders.

"Very nice. You certainly are beautiful, Miranda," he sighed, his hands sliding through her hair. Miranda turned her head aside again, her mind whirling as she tried to figure out what to do. This was a once-in-a-lifetime opportunity, and she couldn't afford to blow it.

"You shouldn't wear such long skirts, you know," Bauer said. "Many young women in the firm wear mini skirts, you know, or the next thing to them. It tends to distract the men, but then that's not always a bad thing." he chuckled. "I bet you have great legs."

"I... wouldn't know," she said.

He slid her hem up her thighs, and she tensed, holding her breath.

"Wonderful legs," he said. He let the hem drop a few inches below her crotch, then his hand slid through her hair again.

"Mister Bauer," she gulped.

"Don't be a shy little girl, Miranda," he breathed. He slid

his right hand under her chin, tilted her head to face him, and kissed her. At first, she drew back, but his other hand was behind her head and held her in place. She pressed her hands against his chest but did not really resist.

You'll be working for a woman, not for him, she thought to herself. What he does now doesn't matter.

His hand slid into her jacket, cupped her left breast, and gently squeezed it. She closed her eyes and trembled.

She thought about how stunned the male students at her dorm were when they heard she had received an invite to an interview there and how jealous they all would be if she got accepted. She also thought about how superior they always acted and how bad they would get if she was turned down here.

Bauer's fingers undid the top three buttons down the front of her blouse, then parted it, gazing inside at the lacy white half-bra and how her soft white flesh strained against it. He slid his fingers inside her blouse and stroked the top of her breasts. He continued kissing her, his tongue pushing against her unyielding lips. With each passing second, she was gripped by the urge to slap him and jump up, but she resisted it, desperately trying to figure out how to fend him off and still get hired here.

His one hand gripped her hair more firmly, pulling it back against the back of the seat. His other hand cupped her breast more firmly, kneading the supple flesh through her thin bra. He slid his hand down and tugged at her blouse, pulling it out from her skirt, then slipped behind her and undid her bra catch.

She folded her arms across her chest and sat forward suddenly, gasping as she tore her lips from his. He sat up as well, his hand still not abandoning its hold on her hair but still sliding through it, stroking it as though he were petting her.

His right hand slid up along her thighs and under her skirt.

"Spread those pretty legs, darling," he whispered. She trembled her mind in a daze.

"Come on, dear child. Don't play hard to get. Open your legs for me."

Still, she sat frozen.

"Open them," he snapped. Her legs jerked open, and she gasped in shock at herself and what she was doing.

"That's a good girl," he breathed, "Just a little wider, baby."

His hand slid up and down her inner thighs, then cupped her pussy mound through her panties. He squeezed her mound, rubbing his hand up and down it, forcing his fingers under her. She sat as if frozen, staring at the wall across the room.

He tugged at her panties, then shoved her back against the back of the couch and jerked her panties down over her hips, legs and off over her white pumps. She stared at them in stunned amazement but could still not look at him.

His hand fumbled at her skirt, undid it, and jerked it down as well, leaving her naked below her blouse. Suddenly he pushed her aside, his body pressing her back against the seat, tilting her sideways, then pushing her onto her back. He was atop her, her legs spread as he settled between them.

She stared at the ceiling now, almost in shock. She numbly ignored his actions as he opened her shirt the rest of the way and began groping her breasts with heavy hands. He gripped her thighs and forced her legs wider, then she felt his cock pushing against her pussy lips.

He entered her, his organ probing inside her fuck tube,

then slowly driving down to the bottom. His weight was heavy atop her as he sighed with pleasure and mashed his groin into her crotch. He kissed her, his tongue darting in between her unresponsive lips.

His hands fingered her nipples, then he bent and began sucking on her left nipple, gnawing on it and rasping his tongue back and forth across the little bud. His hips rubbed from side to side as he ground himself into her, content with his fuck stick sheathed inside her.

He spent long minutes sucking, licking, and fondling her breasts, then began kissing her again and started to hump into her. The couch's springs made it simple to set up a steady rhythm as his cock pumped in and out of her tight little cunt tube. His ass rose and fell, still encased in his expensive pants.

While she was almost naked, he had only unzipped his pants. He slobbered over her nipples, then rose and gripped her thighs, shoving her legs back against her chest. He began to pump into her with hard, deep strokes, her cunt aching from the force of his violent fucking motions.

His hips slammed against her buttocks as he pounded his fuck meat down into her belly. She was crushed together beneath him, folded like an accordion, helpless to do anything as his heavy body slammed her into the couch repeatedly.

She fought back a sob, more from the humiliation she felt than the aching in her cunt, and bit her lip as she waited for him to finish. Never had she felt so cheap and used, and only a narrow, razor-thin margin of control stopped her from screaming and clawing his face, then running home and giving up law altogether.

His cock was pumping faster and faster as Bauer used the springs to increase the force of his strokes. Miranda was squashed into the couch but bounced up and down underneath him as his cock pistoned inside her belly.

Her legs were mashed down into her fat titties, the round meat squished out around them, hard and tight against the straining skin.

"Ohhhh Fuuuuuck!" he gasped. "You tight little slut!"

I'm not a slut, she thought, dazed.

He was panting and gasping for breath, yet he stopped suddenly and glanced at his watch. She wondered if he had another girl on her way, another law student who would be offered the job if she fucked him. Was she doing this for nothing? Would he just send her away even though she'd fucked him? And what will you do if he does? Complain? she thought bitterly.

He rolled off her and pulled her up to a sitting position on the couch, then raised her to her feet and turned her around. He pushed her onto the sofa, her knees on the edge as she leaned forward. She felt the full weight of her tits drop below her as she gripped the back of the couch.

"Spread your legs more, baby," he ordered, "and raise that pretty little ass higher."

She felt his cock probing at her cunt, then it thrust up into her, and he gripped her hips as he began to fuck her even harder than he had before. Miranda was not very experienced at sex. She'd had sex only four times so far, twice in the back of cars, once on a couch, and once in a bed. All four times, she had been on her back, and none of the guys who had fucked her had been nearly as unrestrained as John Bauer Sr.

She knew she was not in an abnormal position, of course, yet felt herself burn with embarrassment at the sight she no doubt presented to the man behind her. It was degrading and horrible, yet she could do nothing else. She had gone too far now to protest. Even as his hips hammered into her soft buttocks, she knew she would do anything he ordered to get this job.

His cock sawed back and forth over her cunt lips with amazing speed. She'd never imagined someone could or would fuck her with such speed and force. Her cunt ached, and her buttocks would surely have bruises after this. She wondered if she'd be able to sit down properly.

Her heavy tits swung back and forth between her as his body pounded into hers. They swung and jiggled and bounced until he gripped them with his hands. His fingers sunk into the fleshy meat, cupping the oozing flesh in widespread fingers.

He twisted and squeezed her tits, mashing and kneading the sensitive flesh, pinching the nipples, twisting them around in circles. His cock continued to drive into her with brutal power, slicing in and out of her fuck pipe with total disregard for her.

"Ungh! Ungh!" he gasped, his hips beating at her buttocks with furious hammering strokes. She could hardly see straight, her body jerking to and fro under the brutal impact of his body.

Then he settled down, his strokes slowly stopping.

"Ahhhhh," he sighed. "Nice pussy."

His cock lay within her for a minute, then he pulled out and gripped her arm, turning her and sitting her on the edge of the couch.

"The job pays five hundred a week," he sighed, standing before her, his cock drooping near her face. "Do well, and you'll return the next few summers. If your work is good enough, you'll be taken on as an associate when you graduate."

He held his flaccid cock against her lips.

"Clean this off, woman," he grinned.

Her lips opened, and he pushed his cock between them.

"Lick it, baby. Suck it."

She felt like throwing up. She felt like killing herself. She began to suck his cock, though, licking it as it lay nestled within her mouth. He held her head in both hands, not forcefully. She took his whole cock into her mouth, sucking as her tongue moved up and down its length.

To her horror, it began to harden. That was the very last thing she wanted. He pumped it slowly, even though it was only half erect, then pulled it out of her mouth after a minute.

His hands pushed her blouse and jacket over her shoulders as he shifted closer and spread his legs, lowering his crotch.

"I've always wanted to tit-fuck a big set of melons," he said.

He ran his cock over her tits, rubbing the glistening wet head against her nipples.

"Push your tits together around it, baby," he ordered. "Come on, I'm sure you've done it before."

She had never done it before, considering it too degrading, but she let her arms press against the sides of her breasts, squeezing them around his cock as he humped slowly forward, sliding the wet fuck stick up and down in her cleavage.

He put one knee on the edge of the couch, getting a better angle for his cock strokes. He turned her to one side and began to grunt in pleasure as he ran his hardening cock in and out of her malleable tit flesh.

"Squeeze those tits, baby," he sighed. "Squeeze em' around my cock."

The door opened suddenly, and both turned as a blonde woman in her twenties walked in.

"John, I have those... Oh my God!" Her eyes widened as

she saw them. A man came in behind her, and he, too, stared at the two.

Miranda shrieked and twisted away, trying to cover herself with her arms. She pulled her jacket around her and her legs up to her chest, her skin beet red as the two people looked down at her.

"What is the meaning of this?" the man demanded in a furious voice.

"Uh, sir, Uh, I uh..." John stuttered.

"Who is this?" The man demanded.

"This, uh, this is a new law clerk, here for the summer from Davis Law."

"She's fired, and I'll personally talk with the Dean about the kind of students they have."

The man stormed out of the room, leaving Miranda staring at the door in wide-eyed terror.

"Poor baby," the blonde woman sighed.

"He's a friend of the Dean, and he is such a prude, you know. He'll probably expel you."

"But I... but I..."

"Should have thought about it before you decided to fuck yourself into a job," the woman sniffed. She left, closing the door behind her.

"Ahh, shit," Bauer grumbled.

"What am I going to do?" Miranda whimpered.

"Ever considered McDonald's?" he grinned. She looked up at him in shock.

"Well, I'm sure you can get into another college. It isn't the end of the world."

"I have a scholarship to Davis," she whispered.

"Oh? Oh well. That's too bad," he shrugged.

She began to whimper, sniffling and rubbing her eyes as tears started to form.

"Oh, don't snivel," he sighed. "Look, I'll talk to the old man. Maybe I can get him to reconsider. Wait here for a couple of minutes."

He left the room. Miranda dressed quickly, the room spinning around her as she contemplated the end of everything she'd worked for. Without a doubt, her expulsion from Davis would bar her from any other college, especially a law school. She'd have to go home, get a job as a secretary – or something.

She huddled in a miserable ball at the edge of the couch for long minutes, praying that John Bauer Sr. could do something to keep her from getting expelled. Maybe she could talk to the man. Maybe... maybe if she fucked him, he wouldn't tell the Dean.

Bauer returned and closed the door behind him, giving her an odd look.

"Meyer is a cold-hearted bastard," he said. He doesn't do anything for nothing. If you want to keep from getting expelled, you will have to do little favor for him."

"He wants to fuck me too," she said, her head threatening to explode.

"No, not quite. Look, you don't know anything about the politics of this place, but to say they're vicious is an understatement. His enemy is Ms. Rogers. You'll have to go and work for her and do whatever he tells you to, get her in trouble. She's his enemy, and you'll have to help us force her out of the firm."

"But, how? I don't know... "

"Ms. Rogers is an evil bitch, to say the least. She's as nasty a sort as you'll ever want to meet. There should be all kinds of things you can find out as her assistant that can get her canned. Besides, she's a lesbian, so maybe she'll make a few passes at you. If we can catch her and you together, they'd get rid of her. They hate homosexuals."

"You mean... you mean you want me to... to sleep with her?" she gasped, horrified.

"Why not? You screwed me for a job. You should be willing to do a little cunt licking to keep it and to keep from getting expelled."

"I couldn't!"

"You could. It's pretty easy to do. We only need enough information to convince the other senior partners that she isn't fit to be among their exalted presence."

"But I'm not gay," she cried, bursting into tears.

"So fake it," he glared. "What's the big deal? Let her suck your tits, suck hers, and lick her pussy. Any idiot can do that, even a big-titted blonde bimbo like you."

The door opened, and the blonde woman came in, closing it behind her.

"So, I see we're going to have a new colleague," she said, her face filled with amusement and scorn.

"Alicia Porter, Miranda Bonner."

"Charmed," Alicia sneered. Miranda reddened.

"She doesn't think she can go along with licking old spider woman's pussy," John laughed. Miranda turned an even darker shade of red.

"Why don't you go and do something, John, while I have a little chat with Miranda."

"Of course, my sweet." He left, and Alicia moved over to perch on the desk, staring at the trembling girl without sympathy.

"Listen to me, you little whore. Benjamin Meyer will make the senior partners table within a month and take me with him, making me a partner. I'll do anything I have to to get that partnership, and that includes fucking the pig." Miranda's eyes widened, and Alicia nodded.

"Yes, that's right, I had to fuck him, have to fuck him. He's a filthy, cruel, rotten, nasty, fucking creep. Just like John thinks he is. John is small-time, though. He's a snotty punk compared to Meyer and Rogers. You will have to do what I'm doing, use your cunt to keep from getting screwed." She laughed and shook her head.

"Look, Miranda, it's no big thing. Do what Meyer wants, and Rogers will be out of here within a month. Then he'll probably ignore you. You'll be an associate here in a couple of years, and I can help you make a partner."

"But I'm not gay or anything. I've never... never done anything..."

"So what?" Alicia growled. "You think I enjoy sucking Meyer's dick? Do you think I like the way he uses me? You put up with what you have to in this business to get ahead. I intend to become rich, little girl, and if you don't want to flip burgers at McDonalds, you'll play along, just like I do."

"Oh, God!" Miranda sobbed, holding her face with both hands.

"Don't be dramatic. It's not like it will hurt. Just play around with the old bitch a little, and that'll be it."

"I don't know if I can!" Miranda cried, staring at her angrily. "I... if she were... I don't know what I'd do. I might... scream or run or... I don't know. I've never done anything with a woman. I don't know how I'd react if she started groping me."

"You seemed to be coping with John pretty well."

Miranda blushed furiously.

"At least he's a man," she sobbed.

"That's a matter of opinion."

"I'll... I'll do what I can," Miranda said bleakly.

Alicia looked at her suspiciously, frowning in thought. What if the little cunt did scream when Ellen grabbed her pussy? That would sure fuck up their plans.

"Shit," she said.

She went to the door and locked it, then reached down and gripped the hem of her dress, pulling it up and over her shoulders, tossing it on the couch as Miranda stared at her in shock.

"Get your clothes off, honey. We're going to have a fast lesson in gay love."

She undid her bra, then stepped out of her panties. Miranda just stared at her, frozen in place like a statue.

"Come on, get undressed. I haven't got all day."

"What... what are you doing?" Miranda gasped.

"Well, I'm not exactly an expert in these things, honey, but when I was at boarding school long ago, one of my girlfriends and I got a little... close for a few months. I can show you what to do and ensure you don't jump out of your skin when the spider woman grabs your tits."

She folded her arms and glared down at the stunned girl.

"Come on, strip," she scowled.

5 – The Teacher

Miranda still didn't move. Alicia clicked her tongue and bent over, yanking the girl to her feet. She began unbuttoning her shirt, her fingers moving quickly down the line of buttons. Miranda jerked back, her arms folded against her chest.

"Do you want Meyer to call the Dean at Davis, or do you want to be a wealthy lawyer?" Alicia glared. She jerked Miranda's arms away and finished unbuttoning her blouse, then shoved it and her jacket off over her shoulders. Miranda dropped her head as Alicia deftly slipped her bra catch and pulled it forward off her, letting her fat tits push free.

"You sure got a nice pair there," Alicia sniffed. She dropped the bra, unzipped Miranda's skirt, and slid it down. She pulled down her panties, and Miranda stepped out of them.

"There now, let's get this over with. Oh, come on, honey. It won't hurt you," she sighed.

She tilted Miranda's face up and smiled at her.

"This can be fun, you know. Me and my girlfriend had fun at it."

She brushed the loose blonde hair out of Miranda's face and smiled in encouragement.

"I'll just show you what to do, so you can handle yourself around Rogers. Okay?"

Miranda gulped and then nodded weakly, her eyes blinking rapidly.

Alicia gripped her shoulder and squeezed it.

"Okay?" she said.

Miranda gave her a weak smile in reply.

"Kiss me," Alicia said. Miranda stared at her anxiously.

"Come on! I won't bite. Kiss me! You already know how to kiss, at least."

Miranda stepped up on her toes and chastely kissed her on the cheek.

"Not like I'm your mother," Alicia glared.

Chastened, Miranda kissed her on the lips, fighting an urge to run. She was leaning forward and trying to keep her tits from making contact with Alicia and trying to keep any part of her from touching Alicia's tits.

"Put your arms around me and kiss me," Alicia ordered.

"I... I don't know..."

Alicia put her arms around the smaller blonde and pulled her in tight. Miranda gasped and squirmed briefly, then held still, her tits mashed into Alicia's as the taller woman held her up on her toes. She blushed furiously, mortified at feeling Alicia's hot tit meat against her own sweating orbs.

"Now kiss me," Alicia said.

Miranda kissed her tentatively, sliding her lips against Alicia's. Alicia pushed her tongue out and into Miranda's mouth, and the little blonde jerked back but was held by Alicia's arms.

She controlled herself and let the other woman slide her tongue in and out her mouth. Alicia's hands slid down her back and cupped her buttocks, squeezing the soft flesh as she pulled Miranda up against her.

"Put your arms around me and squeeze my ass," Alicia said.

"I... I couldn't!"

"Do it!"

Still blushing furiously, Miranda slid her arms around

Alicia, her hands sliding down onto the woman's round buttocks and resting there lightly.

"Squeeze them," Alicia snapped.

Miranda began squeezing her ass cheeks, her mind dazed at what was happening.

Alicia pushed her back a little.

"Kiss my breasts, and suck my nipples. You've had it done to you, I know. Do the same to me. Act like you're the man."

Miranda moaned, her eyes staring at Alicia's high firm breasts.

"Squeeze them, rub them with your hands, and then start sucking my nipples," Alicia said, slightly husky. She gripped Miranda's hands and pulled them up against her breasts, pressing them into her soft flesh.

Miranda swallowed repeatedly, her eyes wide as she stared at her hands on Alicia's tits. Alicia rubbed them around her tits in slow circles, then let them go. Miranda continued rubbing her tits, watching the nipples harden before her eyes.

"Suck them," Alicia said throatily.

Miranda pushed her tongue out between her lips and leaned forward. She hesitated, halting millimeters from Alicia's left nipple. Her tongue slid back into her mouth, and she pulled back, but then she leaned forward again and kissed Alicia's nipple.

Her tongue slid out, and she rasped it slowly across the center of the swollen tit, slurping over the hard nipple. She stared at it, then licked it again, then again. Her hands were cupping Alicia's breasts, her fingers kneading the flesh almost instinctively.

She kissed the nipple again and then sucked, drawing the nub between her lips as she began suckling like a baby. She felt Alicia's hands stroking her head as she sucked and felt oddly comforted.

Alicia leaned back against the desk as Miranda sucked and licked at her nipples. She suddenly whirled around, pressing Miranda back against the side of the desk. She gripped the girl's head and mashed her lips against the startled woman, shooting her tongue into Miranda's mouth.

Her right hand darted between Miranda's legs and gripped her pussy firmly, half lifting her back onto the desk. She stroked and squeezed Miranda's cunt pad as their tongues slithered together. Miranda gasped and moaned as her lips came free, then she stared in wonder as Alicia bent and began sucking on her big left nipple.

It was hard and firmly erect as the older woman folded her lips around it. She sucked hard and worked one of her fingers into Miranda's tight pussy.

"Alicia," Miranda gulped anxiously.

Alicia gripped her thighs and lifted suddenly, shoving her back onto the desk. She parted the girl's slender thighs and stared down at her pussy. Miranda trembled and stared up at her, whimpering anxiously as Alicia bent lower and fingered her twat.

She gripped the edge of the desk as Alicia pried her cunt lips open and then began to lick at her pink pussy meat.

"Ahhhhhh," she gasped.

Alicia's tongue danced across her flesh, slithering over her clitty, then dipping in and out of her hole. She thrust a finger up into her, then a second, and began to pump them in and out as she tongued her clitty.

Miranda let her head fall back against the desk, staring at the ceiling. She felt the heat building within herself, despite her efforts to resist. At first, she was horribly embarrassed, worrying that Alicia would find out, but then it became apparent that her supposed teacher was more than slightly aroused herself.

She moaned, shuddering, as a wave of pleasure washed over her. Her legs pulled further apart, and she slid her hands under her breasts, massaging them discretely. She watched as Alicia's tongue slid back and forth over her clitty, matching the sudden bursts of pleasure with the movement of the wet pink tongue.

Her groin humped up as a spasm of sexual heat ripped through her belly. She squeezed her breasts harder, openly mashing the sent flesh with her fingers. Her buttocks ground down to the edge of the desk as her breathing became harsher, more ragged.

Alicia pulled her mouth off and leaned over the desk, pumping her fingers rapidly in Miranda's pussyhole. She kissed Miranda, mashing her breasts onto the rounded pillows atop the other woman's chest. She threw a leg across Miranda's body, rubbing her pussy over the younger blonde's sweating flesh as she pumped her fingers faster.

Her thumb pressed on Miranda's clitty, grinding it beneath as she worked her fingers inside her snatch. She rolled the hot little button between her thumb and fingers, squeezing tightly as Miranda moaned and humped up repeatedly.

Their lips met in a hot, wet, passionate kiss, the lesson forgotten as their lust exploded in wild carnal desire. Their hot, moist breasts rolled together like dough, and their hands stroked and squeezed each other's bodies.

"Ooohhhh! Ooohhhhh!" Miranda groaned. Alicia pumped her fingers rapidly, rolling and squeezing her clitty as she rubbed her pussy against Miranda's thigh. Miranda came first, though, arching her back and gurgling in wondrous pleasure, her head rolling beneath her as she gripped Alicia's hand and jammed it tightly into her crotch.

Alicia crawled onto the desk and twisted around, her knees coming down on either side of her head. She lowered her cunt, sighing in pleasure as she felt it contact Miranda's face. Miranda's hands pushed up on her buttocks, then her tongue began to probe at the entrance to her fuck box.

She eased her body down onto Miranda, sliding her tongue up and down the hot, wet cunt lips, sawing it between, then prying the tight lips apart and lapping furiously at the glistening flesh inside. She felt Miranda's fingers at her cunt, emulating her, poking her sex lips apart as her tongue pushed inside.

She gasped in pleasure as Miranda's tongue probed at her cunt hole, then drove inside.

"Ohhhhh, yeeeeesss! Ooohhh, baaaabbyyyyy," she sighed, massaging Miranda's thighs. Her hands gripped the little blonde's thighs and opened them wider, then dug into her cunt meat as she hungrily devoured the gleaming wet pink flesh.

Miranda grunted and moaned and whined in heat and confusion and helpless lust. She had never had anyone do such awful, obscene, terrible things to her. Why, Alicia had jerked her off, had masturbated her to an orgasm, and then had licked her to another, had actually eaten her, as the boys used to say.

She had heard that boys, that men, really, would eat girls, but it had always been the other way around in her experience. No man had ever offered to eat her, and she had always been too shy to ask, though she had sucked cocks.

The feel of Alicia's tongue against her slit was just too

much to bear, and it drove all thinking, especially about what was right, proper, or moral right, out of her mind. She became a thing of impulses and instincts, a raw, sexual animal that lived and breathed for pleasure, and the hot, burning core of bubbling energy between her legs.

She squeezed and massaged Alicia's ass while her tongue slurped at her pussy and her nose rooted against her cunt hole. She had never felt so wild, unrestrained, utterly carnal, and sexually free. Never had she imagined she would ever do anything like this. The very idea of what she was doing was so exciting and lewd that it would have made her tremble with lust even without the busy, sucking mouth gnawing on her clitty.

She tried to imitate Alicia, doing to her pussy what the older woman did to hers. Every touch of her tongue and fingers made the little blonde more excited. She also marveled at the sight of Alicia's drooling fuck hole just inches from her eyes and the feel of it against her lips and tongue.

She loved the taste as her tongue drove deep into Alicia's cunt pipe and scooped out her cunt milk. She loved the smell against her nose, the softness of Alicia's buttocks against her hands, and her breasts pressing down, grinding down against Miranda's belly like two warm, soft pillows.

The door opened a crack, though neither of them noticed. John peered in. It was his office, so why Alicia would imagine he wouldn't unlock it and look in was beyond him.

He'd thought at first she was merely trying to convince the little slut that her life would be better off going along with their plans. As time passed and neither of the blondes came out, he suspected Alicia had trouble convincing her.

Eventually, his curiosity got the better of him, and he

unlocked it and opened the door a bit. Now, his cock straining the expensive fabric of his pants leg, he eased into the room and closed the door behind him, his eyes wide as he looked directly into Alicia's crotch and watched the younger blonde sucking and slurping on it.

He swallowed and stumbled forward. He'd had the hots for her for years, but she'd always ignored him, not considering him important enough. He was torn between getting a camera to get blackmail shots and fucking her. His cock won out over his brain, and he lurched against the side of the desk and dropped his pants.

The younger woman saw him but ignored him in her lust to suck on Alicia's fuck hole. John took out his fuck pole and pointed the hard nose against Alicia's snatch, then gripped her hips and pushed himself into her. She grunted but made no move to turn around, too busy sucking on Miranda's hot hole.

John groaned as inch after inch of his bloated fuck stick slid through the straining cunt lips and down into Alicia's belly. Her ass was bouncing and jerking and quivering, and he held it as steady as he could until his cock was buried inside her.

Miranda began licking at his balls, and he closed his eyes and groaned in delight. He began to slowly withdraw his cock from inside Alicia's tight snatch. Miranda's tongue slid along the underside of his cock shaft as it emerged, pushing his lust up another notch.

He thrust back into Alicia, satisfied to hear a grunt from her as his wood smashed deep into her guts. He drew his cock back, sliding it free like he was drawing a sword from a sheath. He pulled the head out through her cunt lips, letting them snap shut, and then pushed his cockhead forward again, but down a couple of inches, pushing it through Miranda's open lips.

His cock slid smoothly down into her mouth and right down her throat. She grunted and then made some wild jerking movements as though that was a big surprise. Indeed, it was a big surprise to him. Her head and throat and his cock were at just the right angle for a straight line down her throat.

He pumped his cock up and down her throat tube several times, then withdrew entirely, and on his next forward stroke, he pushed the head through Alicia's cunt lips and buried his sword inside her belly once again. Miranda began slurping at his balls again and then suddenly shuddered and began to bounce wildly on the desk. Her head jerked from side to side, and she grunted and gurgled in pleasure, her eyes clenched tightly and her mouth open wide. John could not resist drawing his cock out of Alicia and shoving it right down Miranda's throat, stilling all her cries and whimpering moans.

He fingered Alicia's pussy and fucked his prick inside Miranda's throat. He drove three fingers into the slit beneath her humping, grinding ass, pumping them in and out as he searched through her pussy lips for her clitty, found it, then began rubbing and squeezing it. Alicia thrust and humped her ass back at him as he fucked her with his fingers and fucked Miranda's throat with his dong.

Miranda's head fell back to the desk, almost over the edge, actually, and he drew his cock out of her throat and past her lips, then drove it up into Alicia's fuck hole once again. Now he seized her hips and began to fuck her with long, hard strokes, his hips slapping against her ass cheeks as he rutted against her.

She drew her face out of Miranda's crotch and turned around to stare at him through dazed, bleary eyes.

"Bas... bas... tard," she panted. "Bassssstaaarrrd."

"You got it, Alicia," he grunted. "Shake that ass, baby."

"Fuck... you fucker... Bas... bastard," she groaned and humped back against him. "Fuck me! Fuck me! Fuck me!" she whined. "Ungh! Ungh! Ungh!"

He hammered into her buttocks, his hands sliding up and down her sides, moving beneath her to cup and grope her wobbling, shaking tits. She whimpered and rutted back against him, gripping his hands tightly and mashing them harder against her swollen melons.

John freed one hand and slid it down her belly, jamming it between her legs and fingering her clitty. He pushed it down against his pumping cock shaft, drawing a squeal of pleasure and a series of grunts and moans from the haughty blonde.

Miranda began licking at her clitty again, pushing up on her belly to keep from getting her face mashed down flat as the other blonde jerked and bounced over her. Her tongue lapped at Alicia's fuck button, licking over it, as well as John's finger and cock.

Alicia began to climax, shaking her ass furiously, yelping and grunting and whining in bliss. John gripped her hair and pressed her face into Miranda's cunt, muffling her cries of pleasure. He skewered her with furious thrusts, humping her jerking, shuddering body, ripping his cock up and down her fuck tunnel, gripping her ass, and fondling her tits.

As Alicia collapsed, he was torn between a desire to keep fucking her and the urge to stuff his cock back down into Miranda's throat. He kept pumping, wanting to drop his load inside Alicia's pussy as he'd wished for years, wanting to know, as he looked at her for the rest of the day, that she had his jism up inside her.

He came then, each beat of his wildly pounding heart sending another thick, gooey wad of cock cream into her snatch. He groaned. His hands gripping her flanks tightly as he rammed himself up her hole to the balls and then held himself against her, locked against her buttocks.

"You sonovabitch," Alicia groaned.

"Yeah, I am that," he sighed, slowly drawing his cock back down her fuck tube.

* * *

To say Ellen was pleased when presented with her new law clerk would have been an understatement. She hid it well, but inside she felt a convulsive lurch, a hot, steamy explosion of lust.

The sweet-faced little blonde wore a high-necked white collar and a navy blue jacket with white pants. Her golden hair delightfully flowed over her shoulders. She was adorable! Ellen knew she had to have her, no matter what it took. She figured it was probably too much to hope for that the sweet child was gay, but whether she was or not, Ellen intended to have her eating pussy as soon as possible. After all, she was a senior partner in one of the nation's most prestigious firms. This little chit could be induced to do almost anything for a promise of her backing to get herself hired after she graduated.

Unless she was one of those strange, naive fools, who thought you should try and work your way up the ladder without help, strictly on the merits of your work. If so, she would quickly disillusion the child.

And the child is what she was, or at least, what she looked

like. Put on a tartan skirt below that navy jacket, and Ellen might have mistaken her for a high school girl. I'll have to keep her under tight control, Ellen thought, before one of these bastards manages to get their pricks into that tight little pussy.

She wondered if the girl was a virgin. That would really be too much to hope for these days, though she'd popped many a girl's cherry in the past with one of her dildos. The little blonde was young, though, and probably hadn't been fucked very often, only by fumble-fingered teenage boys. Ellen intended to turn her, to drive her wild with orgasms, and convince her that lady love was the only way to go.

She put on her most convincing smile and set about charming the girl, letting her know how powerful, wealthy, and intelligent she was and how much help she could be in Miranda's future career.

The girl seemed nervous, but that was only to be expected, and besides, Ellen was busily plotting how to get her out of those clothes. Should she try it herself or let one of her little helpers set it up? If the girl screamed and went telling tales, it would be better if she couldn't implicate her. Still, she wanted to seduce her. Seducing virgins, girls who'd never been fucked by a woman, was delightful and rewarding. She remembered that stubborn little teenager who once lived next door to her. Ellen had been as sweet, loving, caring, and understanding with the girl as she'd been capable of, yet none of her hints had produced anything. All she'd succeeded in doing was becoming the girl's big sister confessor. And the girl's confessions had been far too concerned with her puppy love with boys. That had infuriated Ellen. She'd had the girl raped one day, paying the punk to be as cruel, nasty, and sadistic as he could be without harming her.

The girl had turned to Ellen for comfort, having no mother, but despite the fear of men the attack had brought out in her, she was still hesitant about accepting Ellen as her lover. More potent medicine had been called for. Ellen had, had her gang raped over a long weekend. She'd watched secretly as the girl was raped, sodomized, degraded, and tormented in every way, reduced to a sniveling, mindless, huddled-up ball of flesh.

And then she showed such great love and devotion after the girl exited the hospital that she melted into her arms. She'd been sorry not to be able to pop her cherry with the dildos but had enjoyed her devotion for years afterward until some damned shrink had gotten into the act and cured her fear of men.

Now the little whore was a mother out in the suburbs, with five kids, no less. By chance, she had spotted the family at a theatre last month. The woman's oldest girl was a scrumptiously pretty twelve-year-old. She had decided then and there to wait a couple of years, then seduce her away from her mother. That would show the ungrateful whore.

But that afternoon, as she helped Miranda adjust to her role and duties as her law clerk, she enjoyed the mere sight of the luscious little morsel and was tormented by it. She used every opportunity to contact her, patting her back or shoulder and touching her hand or hair.

She invited her out after work for a get-together drink. To her happiness, the girl had accepted, though she'd informed Ellen that she wasn't yet old enough to drink.

"Don't worry about that tonight, honey," Ellen purred. "We'll go to my club. They won't care there."

In fact, her "club" was a very expensive, exquisitely decorated, and luxuriously appointed one that catered strictly to the wealthy women in the city's business district. It had a long waiting list of women wishing to join, few of whom had any idea that the membership was restricted to gay or bisexual women.

The smartly dressed woman at the door did not question Miranda's age, nor did the equally well-appointed young lady tending the sleek, leather, and oak bar. Miranda's nervousness might have been allayed if she'd known that the club had seen many "women" far younger than herself, all playtoys of the wealthy elite who comprised the membership.

Miranda looked around with starry eyes as Ellen, all friendship and warm smiles, introduced her to the elegant lounges with their fireplaces, the sleek, high-tech chrome and carpet exercise rooms, the racquetball courts, the indoor tennis courts, squash courts, and the many famous, renowned women who were members.

She also blushed nicely when Ellen showed her the indoor Olympic pool, the hot tubs, the saunas, and the massage rooms, most probably because the women in all these areas were quite nonchalantly nude.

She wanted to impress the girl, and she succeeded. Miranda was awed by what she saw and treated her boss with admiration and reverence.

Normally Ellen would wait, choosing a slow, careful seduction. The sweet little blonde was such a delectable morsel, with that pretty face and big, firm-looking breasts, that she could hardly keep her hands off the girl.

"What we need is some physical exercise to take our minds

off all that legal crap we've been wading through today," Ellen said. "What would you like?"

"Oh, gosh, Ms. Rogers, I'm so tired now I don't think I could do anything."

"Miranda, my dear, you only think you're tired," Ellen smiled, patting her shoulder. "It's your mind that has been working hard today. Your body hasn't done a bit. You can easily fall into a rut like that, letting your body go to the pot. That's why an exercise club is so important. You need physical exercise to keep from getting flabby. Let's play a little racquetball, shall we?"

"But I don't know how, and anyway, I didn't bring any clothes."

"I'll be delighted to show you, my dear, and as for clothes," she waved her hand dismissively. "The club has plenty of clothes that are available on request. I'm sure we can find you something... appropriate."

6 – The Health Club

The club was happy to lend Miranda a green tank top and a pair of short nylon shorts. The shorts were tight, as was the tank top, but they fit. Ellen hadn't had to tell them what to do; the women at the club had seen this kind of thing many times before and would help in any way they could.

Miranda was not very good at racquetball, though Ellen patiently showed her how it was done. She went easy on the little blonde, though she did make sure she had to dive and run for all her shots. The tight nylon shorts pulled into her crack several times, and Miranda continuously tugged them down.

Miranda's big boobs bounced up and down in the tight tank top. Knowing that would happen, she'd wanted to wear her bra, but Ellen had been gently persuasive. After all, the tank top had big armholes, and her bra straps would be quite visible, which would be gauche. That the sides of her tits were now quite visible through those same armholes was beside the point. The club was women-only. Who would care?

She ran the blonde around the court, then put a comradely arm around her shoulders and led her from the court. The women nearby watched with smiles and appreciative looks of hunger on their faces, eyeing the tight little ass and big tits of the blonde. Ellen gave the other women a careful, hands-off look.

"I know what we can do. We'll do a little aerobics," she said, sounding so enthusiastic that Miranda, tired or not, could hardly refuse.

Again the club had a suit to loan her. It was pretty tight

against her breasts and equipped with a pair of pink tights. The tights were a necessity since the suit had only a narrow strip of material up between the buttocks, leaving them completely free.

She'd never worn one before and was rather shy, especially bending over. There was another woman in the row behind her who would have a great look at her ass and the tight, straining material across her cunt pad. She reassured herself that the other women were all dressed alike, and as Ellen said, they were all girls here.

After the aerobics, Ellen led the exhausted girl to the massage rooms. She had forgotten the women there were unclothed for their massages, and so, despite her weariness, she was pretty self-conscious as she lay on her belly, naked, on a thin table. Ellen lay beside her on another table and seemed oblivious of their nudity.

The two women who began to massage them also seemed unconcerned by it. They both wore white dresses like nurses and had strong fingers as they worked into the tired muscles. The oily fingers and everyone's casual attitude about nudity began to relax Miranda, and she began to actually enjoy the massage.

She grew less comfortable as the woman massaging her worked her hands up the insides of her thighs. She never actually touched her pussy, well, except for brushing across it once or twice by accident, but Miranda was intensely aware of how close her fingers were.

Then Ellen rolled over, and a minute later, Miranda's masseuse told her to roll over. Now she was embarrassed all over again. Still, she couldn't make a fuss. She rolled over, not looking at the woman, or anyone else. She'd always been self-conscious about the size of her breasts.

The woman's face betrayed nothing of her thoughts as she began to work on Miranda's legs again, slowly going up her thighs. She skipped over her pubic mound, though her hands dripped some oil there accidentally, and began to work on her stomach and lower chest. She didn't actually massage her breasts, but her hands moved up and down her sides, brushing the sides of her mounds several times and moving up between them. Getting more oil on them.

Miranda was becoming somewhat aroused by the massage and her nudity to her consternation. The visible sign of that was that her nipples were getting hard. She kept her mouth tightly closed, horribly embarrassed, but the woman made no sign she saw anything unusual.

Miranda turned her head to one side, unable to look at her, and noted Ellen lying flat on the table only a couple of feet away. Ellen, too, was nude, and Miranda could not help noting how powerfully built the tall, raven-haired woman was.

Muscles slid beneath the skin of her arms and legs whenever she moved them and along her tight flat belly. Her breasts were big and firm-looking, perfectly situated and rounded. Of course, they weren't as big as Miranda's, and the woman had a much larger chest to go with them, so they didn't seem so large.

Miranda was acutely conscious of her big, fat, soft melons resting on her slim chest. Of course, they were not as soft as usual because they were somewhat swollen by her own arousal. She wanted to cover them with her arms, to hide them from the masseuse and Ellen.

"What we need now," Ellen groaned, "is a shower. No, a bit of time in the sauna, then a shower." She rose gracefully and took a towel from her masseuse. Miranda got up as well, half covering her breasts with one arm, before taking a towel from the other woman.

She scurried after Ellen, missing the knowing looks the two masseuses exchanged.

Ellen led her into one of the small, private booths with just two short six-foot-long benches. Once they got inside the steamy room, it became evident that one of the benches was broken in half.

"Oh well, we can use this one, Ellen sighed, removing her towel and sitting down on the one bench. Miranda also sat down, removing the towel only when Ellen asked her questioningly. Ellen began talking about her years in law school, sliding over until her hip was a scant inch from Miranda's. After a few minutes, she put a friendly arm over Miranda's shoulder, thus bringing the side of her left breast up against the side of the young blonde's right. Both pretended not to notice it.

Ellen was as calm as she could be on the outside. Inside she was boiling with lust and exultation. The girl was almost ready! And she was so cute, her body so soft, her flesh so sweet, so well built, with big round, fat tits and a sweet, little behind. The gash between her legs was plainly visible through the soft thatch of golden pussy hair and made Ellen drool with lust.

Miranda was also excited for her part, though not to the same degree. Still, she was breathing fast, butterflies moving around inside her belly at the proximity to the naked woman. She knew what Ellen was and that the woman would make a move on her, and she also knew that she had no choice but to allow her the unrestricted use of her body.

What was strange and puzzling was that she had little

desire to resist. She was growing hotter all the time, and not just because of the heat in the sauna. The sweat dribbling down her belly and between her legs was not all because of the outside heat; some was because of her inner heat.

She almost wished Ellen would do it and get it over with, ending the suspense. She was anxious about being seen here in this semi-public place. She hadn't seen any lock on the door, and the idea of being discovered... again, was terrifying. She'd never been as mortified as she had been the other day when Alicia and Mr. Meyer caught her like that.

"Oooohhh, I've got to stretch out," Ellen groaned, stretching her arms high above her and arching her back. Miranda turned her head to see but quickly jerked it forward again.

Ellen smiled to herself. She leaned away from the younger woman, then pulled her legs up and slid them down the length of the bench behind Miranda. The little blonde shifted her behind forward on the bench to avoid contact with Ellen's legs.

Ellen lay on her side, her head propped up on one hand, eyeing the blonde girl with unconcealed hunger.

"Come lay down, honey. Stretch out those legs," she breathed.

"Uh, no, I'm okay," Miranda gulped.

"Oh, come on. There's plenty of room." Ellen gripped her left wrist and tugged the girl down playfully. Automatically, Miranda's legs rose to counterbalance herself, and she was soon lying on the bench on her side, fighting to stop shaking as she felt her buttocks press against Ellen's hips and groin.

"You're not on the edge? You won't fall off, now, will you?" Ellen asked. Her right hand slid around Miranda's waist and down onto her belly, pulling her back more firmly.

Miranda felt the older woman's breasts pushing into her shoulders and closed her eyes, her breathing coming faster. She waited, but Ellen did nothing, though she kept her arm in place, draped over Miranda's waist.

Despite her lust for the nubile young woman, Ellen was enjoying the hunt too much to finish it quickly. She pressed her breasts harder into her shoulders, delighting in the soft heat of Miranda's skin. She could feel the girl's trembling and knew she was aware of the sexually charged air, anxious, and she hoped, excited.

"You have a lovely body, Miranda," she said softly.

"Thank you," Miranda whispered.

"I bet the men are always coming on to you."

"Sometimes."

"And do they stare at your boobs when you're talking?"

"Sometimes."

"Men are so mad about breasts," she sighed. "Lord knows why. They're really just functional appendages there for child-rearing."

She drew her arm slowly back, letting her hand coast up Miranda's belly and onto her side. She trailed it, light as a feather, down over Miranda's hip and down the outside of her leg. Miranda shivered in response.

"Then again, you do have lovely breasts. They're so large. Aren't they uncomfortable?"

"N... " Miranda cleared her throat. "No," she gulped. "I mean, not usually."

"The bra straps don't dig into your shoulders?"

Ellen trailed her hand back up Miranda's side, over her hip, and up her side to her shoulder, rubbing it lightly.

"Sometimes they do," Miranda breathed.

"Of course, you're young yet, very young. You're breasts are still firm, aren't they? They don't need much support, so I suppose they don't pull down much."

She trailed her hand down the trembling girl's side and over her hip again.

"They're nicely shaped for such large ones," she said. "Many women with large breasts have big cone-shaped ones, all pointy. Yours are so round, just like grapefruits or maybe cantaloupes," she said, her voice warm, amused.

"And your nipples are adorable, not big and round and oval like many women with large breasts. They're pretty neat, small and round and pink, very attractive."

She rose a bit higher on her arm and glanced down the girl's front.

"They certainly are long, too. I noticed that earlier in the massage room. I don't remember when I've seen nipples push out quite so far from breasts. They must be half an inch long."

Miranda didn't know how to respond, so she kept quiet. She flushed with embarrassment, though terribly uncomfortable, as the older woman discussed her breasts.

"Are they very sensitive?" Ellen asked. "I've always wondered; I mean, since your breasts are so large and your nipples are so long."

Miranda was frozen, her body stiff.

"Miranda?"

"Yes," she whispered.

"Are they very sensitive?"

"I... I don't know."

"Well, I'm sure you've had men squeeze and rub them before and suckle off your nipples. Are they very sensitive for being large?"

"I don't know," she squeaked.

"I suppose you don't really have any way to compare that, do you?" Ellen laughed. "How would you know if your nipples were more sensitive than another woman's, no matter how many times they'd been fondled. And anyway, men don't really know much about handling breasts. Have you noticed that? They tend to grab them and squeeze as hard as they can, over and over again."

Miranda admitted to herself that that was, in fact, true. The only person who had ever shown much delicacy with her mammaries was... Alicia.

Ellen trailed her hands along Miranda's neck through her long blonde hair. She shifted it aside, baring the nape of her neck, and rubbed it gently with her fingers. Her hand slid across Miranda's side again, pressing limply against her belly.

"Men really are selfish when they make love," Ellen mused. "They only show consideration for themselves. It's wham bam, thank you, Ma'am, then roll over and get a cigarette. What do they care if the woman doesn't orgasm? Tell me, do you orgasm when a man makes love to you?"

"Uh, uhmmm, I uh, I... some... sometimes," Miranda mumbled.

"I bet they always do, though, every single time. From the time we go through puberty, we're taught that satisfying the male sexual desire is all important. First, we give them hand jobs, then blow jobs, then finally, we let them push their organs inside us and pump away, then spurt their sticky sperm inside us. And what do we get out of it but diseased or pregnant."

She kissed Miranda's neck lightly, then trailed her lips across it. Her hand, the one across Miranda's side, began to stroke her belly, moving in slow, light circles.

"This is so relaxing," Ellen sighed. Her hand circled slowly and eased downwards onto Miranda's abdomen. Miranda didn't move, though her head, still propped up on her hand, trembled more, and her elbow ached as it vibrated against the bench.

Ellen's hand stroked her lower belly, then eased right down her thigh, sliding up and down the inside. She trailed it onto her stomach again, rubbing lightly, then, quite naturally, it seemed, slid it down and directly over Miranda's pussy mound.

She cupped Miranda's lightly furred pussy mound in her hand, squeezing it a little. Miranda lay motionless, all her awareness concentrated on that hand, which was down between her legs and covering her cunt like a cap over a volcano.

Ellen began to rub it up and down, firmly stroking the hyper-sensitive fuck pad. Miranda began to breathe once more, but it was becoming ragged. Ellen's middle finger pressed harder as it slid directly down along Miranda's cunt slit.

The digit finger began to press downward through her tight, protective pussy lips, sawing against her pink skin beneath. She sawed her finger up and down between Miranda's cunt lips, stroking directly across her outraged clitty.

Miranda held her breath as her entire groin began to burn like wildfire out of control. Her mouth opened and closed like a fish, and she gurgled helplessly, trying to fight off the towering wave of orgasmic energy which hovered above her.

She was hardly aware of Ellen's left hand sliding under her, her hand coming up and fastening firmly around her solid, swollen right breast squeezing it softly as her forearm rubbed across her left mammary. All her senses focused on her cunt, on the howling pleasure as it fluctuated wildly up and down, up and down, up and down, echoing the movements of Ellen's finger.

Then she gave a strangled cry of shock, arching her back. She came with a tremendous blast of energy, her hips grinding into the bench as she humped desperately against Ellen's finger in her crotch. Her body shook and jerked spastically, her head rolling back, her eyes closed, her ass slapping helplessly into Ellen's fingers in her groin.

"Ungh! Ungh!" she grunted as her ass humped back furiously.

"There, there," Ellen purred. She squeezed Miranda's fat melons as her finger stroked heavily across her clitoris. Her finger moved in short, rapid motions, frigging Miranda's spasming clitty. She gripped the gift's fat tit tightly, pressing the heel of her right hand into her belly to keep her body pressed tightly against the shuddering young blonde's.

Her lips fastened on the nape of the whimpering girl's neck, and she licked over her flesh as she sucked hard. Her teeth bit down, not gently, as she sucked like a vampire. She ground her own loins into Miranda's slapping, humping buttocks as she held the girl against her through a prolonged orgasm, her mind awash in satisfaction and lust as she felt the young woman's body jerking and shaking.

Mine, she thought, all mine!

She bit down harder on the little blonde's throat, her face pressed tightly into the quaking girl's throat as she continued manipulating her clitoris. She knew she would leave a tremendous hickey behind and exulted in what would be a visible sign of her conquest.

She continued until Miranda's body began to ease its frantic movements. Only then did she ease up, both on the stroking of her clitty and the sucking and chewing of her throat? She let her body move backward until her ass was pressed against the back of the bench, then removed her hand from Miranda's groin and rolled the moaning girl onto her back.

Feeling half dead, Miranda lay there, her left arm hanging limply down off the edge of the bench, her right at her side, pressed against Ellen's hot body.

"Feel better?" Ellen breathed, her face smiling. Miranda didn't answer, merely staring, her chest heaving from exertion. Slowly, as the last remnants of the orgasm passed, she began to darken in embarrassment, shyness returning.

Ellen was still lying on her side, her head propped up on her elbow as she stared down at the prone blonde. Her right hand trailed slowly along Miranda's belly, stroking her flesh as it moved onto her chest. She rubbed at Miranda's full, round mammaries. First, her left, then her right, moving in circular motions around the edges of each breast, then inwards towards the center, though missing the nipples.

She bent her head then and rubbed her cheeks back and forth against the full, firm mounds. After caressing them with her cheeks for long seconds, she turned and slid her tongue across one straining nipple. Her tongue felt the hardness of the sharp little nub and marveled at it.

She slurped away at it slowly, her tongue moving like a tabby cat's as it lapped at Miranda's sensitive nipple. Her hand gently kneaded the breast, distorting its perfect shape briefly, then her lips surrounded the nipple, and she sucked slowly and softly.

She rolled over, half atop the slight blonde, pressing her swollen mounds against Miranda's hot skin. She kneaded the girl's right tit with her left hand as she continued to suck on her left nipple. Her right hand slithered slowly down the girl's belly, caressing her soft flesh, then moving further down and into her groin, cupping her pussy mound.

Helplessly, Miranda humped up at the hand, her cunt startled by the purity of the jagged sexual bolt that ripped into it. Ellen fingered her clitty, her fingers dipping lightly into her fuck tunnel as they rolled back and forth across her fuck button.

She sucked harder on Miranda's left nipple, her cheeks puckered as she drew it higher into her mouth. Her teeth closed around it, grinding from side to side, nipping and pinching as she sucked. Her tongue worked rapidly over the tiny pink bud of flesh as she slowly worked a finger down Miranda's fuck pipe for the first time.

The finger sawed in and out, grinding over her clitty, then pushing deep until her knuckles rubbed against the girl's cunt lips. She twisted her hand from side to side, working the finger around the sides of Miranda's tiny, elastic fuck tube, grinding her knuckles against her pussy mound.

She pumped it in and out, then added a second finger. Her finger pushed up hard against the top of Miranda's fuck pipe, stroking her clitty as her thumb pressed down on the hot little bud from the other side. Her teeth gnawed hungrily at Miranda's left nipple, then left it as the panting woman stared down at the little blonde like she was prey about to be devoured.

She growled and then mashed her face into Miranda's fat tit mound, biting into the flesh on the underside, making the blonde yelp in pain. Ellen's mouth opened and closed repeatedly as she made little bites and nips across the surface of the fat, swollen melon, her teeth snapping and pinching the sensitive flesh.

She focused on the big nipple again, standing so straight and high. Her mouth opened wide and snapped closed on a big hunk of tit meat surrounding the nipple. She sucked as she gnawed at the flesh, her tongue whipping furiously. She twisted her head from side to side, twisting the malleable flesh.

Her fingers pumped faster and faster inside Miranda's fuck tunnel as she diddled her clitty with frenzied thumb motions. Her left hand was repeatedly squeezing the girl's right tit mound, mashing the flesh down, making it ooze out between her long, splayed fingers. Miranda was whimpering and whining, her body wriggling helplessly on the bench as it was inundated by sharp staccato bursts of sensory explosions.

Pain, pleasure, fear, embarrassment, lust, anxiety, delight, awe, and wonder rippled across her bewildered mind as she watched and felt the older woman play with her body.

The pain was slight, though, and fleeting, and the embarrassment was quickly overshadowed by the pleasure and the lust as the lewdness, and carnal nature of the woman's actions aroused her passions to a higher and higher pitch.

She was astonished that, having cum just from Ellen's hand, she was well underway for another orgasm from the same source. Never could she have imagined two short days before that women would be masturbating her to orgasm and that it would feel so good, so much better, so much more marvelous than when she rubbed her little cunt on her own.

Her whimpering grew, and she moaned as her body arched upwards, her cunt humping against Ellen's fingers, her breasts pushing against her lips and hand. Her arm went around

Ellen, pulling her head down against her chest. She grabbed her hand and ground it harder into her cunt.

She made a gurgling cry of passion as she felt her orgasm washing up, flooding her system. Then she lost control of herself as her body came with a shattering crescendo of orgasmic pleasure, her senses overwhelmed by a blastwave of crackling carnal energy that rippled up and down her body, searing her to the core of her being.

Her body writhed, jerked, and shuddered on the bench, almost throwing the heavier woman off. Her head banged painfully into the wood below her, and her arms flopped and jerked spastically as she was buried beneath an avalanche of ecstatic delight. Her muscles spasmed, her back arching again, and her legs flopped and bounced on the bench.

She cried out in delight, in bliss, in ecstatic release as her soul flew high through a hurricane of blinding white light and exploding fireworks. Every portion of her body was rippling with the power of the snapping, burning energy that tore through her.

And then she gave a final, convulsive jerk and fell still, but for her heaving chest and the occasional twitch or tremor, groaning weakly as she sought to regain her breath. Her eyes were narrow slits, and she breathed like a bellows. Her glistening sweat-covered body was limp and washed out on the bench.

"Sweet little darling," Ellen cooed.

7 – The Spectators

Ellen led the dazed young blonde out of the sauna. Miranda was too weary and confused to even care that she was naked as Ellen led her past several admiring women and into a shower stall. The stall offered partial privacy, with a curtain covering everything above their knees.

Miranda stood there submissively as Ellen began to soap her up. Ellen's long, strong fingers soon slid through the slippery soap as they moved over her full, fat breasts, down her smooth, flat stomach, and between her slim thighs.

She rubbed particularly well between the girl's legs, her fingers probing at her cunt tunnel, sliding between her pussy lips and up and down her ass crack. She cleaned Miranda's hair, back, and legs, washing her like a child with her doll.

And then it was Miranda's turn. Covered with soap and somewhat recovered from her enormous cum, she stared up shyly at Ellen's strong, muscular body, then hesitantly began to soap her up. She started with her arms and shoulders, then slid past her breasts to work on her belly.

Ellen gripped her wrists gently and firmly pulled them back onto her breasts. Miranda stared wide-eyed at the full, firm round tit orbs as her fingers kneaded them. She soaped them from side to side, up and down, and in slow, circular motions, swallowing nervously as she did.

Then she continued down Ellen's body, again hesitating over her groin, skipping it to rub her thighs and hips instead. Ellen laughed in amusement, and Miranda blushed. The older woman took Miranda's hand and brought it in between her legs, laying it up flat against her pussy mound.

She rubbed it back and forth several times, then let go. Blushing furiously, Miranda rubbed the other woman's pussy. It was the first time she had ever felt another woman's private sex. She didn't really count Alicia since she had been half-crazed with lust at the time.

Now, coldly aware, she felt every ridge of the woman's cunt crack and the soft little hairs around it. She noted the pulpy, meaty feel of the fuck mound and dipped her fingers in between the cunt lips, recognizing their tightness from her own pussy.

Ellen turned, and Miranda soaped up her shoulders and back, then moved lower. This time she needed no encouragement to rub her hands through the meaty flesh of Ellen's backside. Her fingers dug into the soft ass mounds, soaping up and down. Then, with great daring, she thought, she slid her hand right down the middle of Ellen's ass crack, rubbing across her asshole and down between her legs.

Her hand palmed Ellen's cunt mound, rubbing up and down over it before sliding back up the middle of the woman's ass.

Ellen turned and faced her, backing the smaller, slighter woman against the wall. Miranda swallowed nervously as Ellen's eyes scanned her up and down, then she melted into the woman's arms as Ellen hugged her tightly.

Their soapy bodies slid together in a wet, warm embrace, their fat, slippery breasts mashing and grinding against each other as their lips sought each other. Ellen slid one hand behind the girl's head, pressing her lips tightly against her, and her other hand down between the girl's ass cheeks, squeezing them and pulling her up to her toes against her.

She humped her groin into Miranda, her hand squeezing the girl's crotch, sliding further in between her slippery thighs to cup her cunt mound from behind. She squeezed it up as she forced the younger woman to her toes. Her lips crushed Miranda's, her tongue darting into the other woman's oral cavity.

Miranda's arms and hands were pinned between them momentarily, but she freed her arms, leaving only her hands, which squeezed up against Ellen's titties, kneading them briefly before withdrawing and letting her breasts mash against Ellen's.

Her hands slid behind Ellen, hugging her, aroused despite her two recent orgasms. Her entire body was throbbing with heat as she kissed back as passionately as she could, her tongue meeting Ellen's in a lewd, carnal dance of lust between their mouths.

They circled slowly, in and out of the stream of water, brushing against the walls, almost slipping and falling through the curtain a couple of times. They groaned and sighed in pleasure as they groped and fondled each other's soapy flesh and tasted each other's tongues.

Ellen continued to hold the back of Miranda's head, dominating her movements. Her other hand pulled free from beneath her buttocks, circled, and dove down the girl's belly to grip her cunt. Suddenly she thrust a finger up into the girl, then a second, then a third, pumping hard, forcing them deep.

Miranda grunted in surprise as she was reamed out from beneath. The three soapy fingers stabbed up again and again as Ellen's thumb began to rub quickly across her clit, grinding it back and forth. She pulled back on Miranda's head, sticking her left knee out as she bent the girl backward.

Miranda's legs spread, and she whined and groaned with lust, her hands flailing behind her as Ellen pulled her hair and grabbed her wrist as Ellen sent hard, spearing thrusts up into her cunt. Her coordination was off, and her movements were jerky. Her senses sent conflicting, confusing signals, and she couldn't think straight.

She came again, crying in ecstasy, heedless of who might hear. She humped against Ellen's fingers as the older woman masturbated her to a third, powerful orgasm, wondering, amid the clamoring signals of sensory overload, what was happening to her, what she was becoming.

Ellen washed the soap off both of them and then led the rubber-legged girl out of the shower stall and into the main section of the locker room. She dried her with a fluffy white towel, then dried herself as Miranda stood mutely beside her.

She sat the younger woman down and lovingly dried her hair with a blow dryer, working it into a thick, fluffy mane of golden silk that framed her pretty, round little face. She dried her own hair quickly, then bound it behind her as usual.

She led Miranda out of the locker room. Wearing only robes, the two went down another hall, turned a corner, and moved through the main gym. They took a small, discrete elevator upstairs and emerged in a plushly carpeted hall lined with doors.

This time, Miranda was starting to become embarrassed again about only wearing a robe in a public place, especially since Ellen was holding her by the hand. They didn't have to go any further, though, as Ellen led her through one of the doors.

She found herself in a luxuriously appointed bedroom

with a huge, four-poster bed complete with a canopy. Ellen led her straight to the bed, then turned her around and undid her robe, pulling it open and removing it.

"On the bed, darling," Ellen ordered. Anxiously but willingly, Miranda sat, then lay down on the bed. Ellen slipped off her robe, knelt on the bed, and straddled Miranda's tiny body. She leaned over and kissed her once, then took her hands, pulled them high above her head, and spread them apart.

She sat on Miranda's chest just below her breasts, her thighs pressing firmly into the big tit-mounds as she reached the top of the bed for something. Miranda felt something soft sliding around her left wrist and cocked her head to see.

It was a rope of some kind, a velvet rope perhaps. Ellen tied it lightly but firmly around Miranda's narrow wrist, then reached the other corner of the bed and pulled out a similar velvet rope. She fixed that around Miranda's right wrist, tying it as firmly as the other.

"What are you doing?" Miranda finally worked up the nerve to ask.

"Shhhh. You'll love it, darling. Don't worry."

With her wrists bound to the top corners of the bed, Miranda felt a quiver of fright, though she quickly discarded it. Ellen wouldn't hurt her. She was just playing a game. Still, it worried her a little that she could not do anything to resist whatever Ellen chose to do to her.

But then, she wouldn't have resisted her anyway, she thought to herself.

Ellen pulled her slender legs far apart and tightly bound her ankles to the bed's bottom corners, spread-eagling the nubile young woman before her. Helpless, Miranda felt a wave of eroticism wash over her. She felt so utterly sexual now, so carnal and raw and… and also completely exposed.

Ellen smiled, her eyes like a cat's. She padded across the room and disappeared through a door. For long minutes Miranda was alone, aroused, but flustered, trying to imagine how she had come to such a state as this when she had been a normal if unexceptional law student only two days ago.

She had never engaged in sexual games of this sort. She knew Ellen was a much more sophisticated, intelligent, wealthy, and experienced woman. She was in awe of the woman's strength and discipline and a little frightened of her, wondering if she would find out that Miranda was working against her.

Then Ellen emerged, and her eyes widened, her fears escalating quickly. Ellen looked frightening, her whole, rounded body clad in shining black rubber.

She wore thigh-high, spike-heeled boots that made her seem taller than she already was. Her hair was still bound behind her head, and now she wore a thick, leather collar around her throat covered with metal studs. She wore a tight leather corset that was low cut and squeezed her tits up and together, giving her a deep exposed cleavage. On her hips was a G-string, and on her arms were leather gloves that covered her arms up to the elbows.

The makeup on her face gave her a sinister appearance, dark and forbidding, her smiles seeming evil and dangerous. She held a black leather bag in one hand as she moved towards the bed. She halted at the edge and smiled at the luscious little blonde as she strained at her bonds.

"Little pretty," she breathed, licking her lips.

First, she removed a blindfold from the bag, slipping it over

Miranda's bulging eyes and tying it tightly behind her head. Then she pulled her tools from the bag and set them out on the bed between the girl's legs. She got into bed and knelt there, staring down the length of Miranda's body.

"We'll see how much you can take, little dear," she whispered.

"Ellen, you won't hurt me, will you?" Miranda begged fearfully. Ellen smiled, not replying.

She turned towards the doorway, nodding to her friends Kristin, Valerie, and Charlotte. The three fully dressed women moved slowly into the room and sat down in the chairs around the bed. Ellen was a true artist, and they had come to watch her work on the previously heterosexual girl.

Ellen reached out with her gloved hands and folded them around Miranda's fat breasts, squeezing tightly, mashing the meaty tit orbs up and out like mushrooms as her fingers squeezed them in from the sides.

She let them go and slid a feather along the girl's inner thigh, sliding it up and down one, then the other, skipping over her pussy entirely.

She worked the feather up Miranda's side, making her gasp and strain at her bonds again.

"Oohhh! Oh, don't!" Miranda cried.

Ellen slid the feather up under her arm, and Miranda yelped again. Ellen ignored her. She let the feather caress the girl's bound arm, then moved along her cheek. She picked up a second feather, sliding it under the girl's other arm, down through her armpit, and down the side of her chest.

Again she ignored Miranda's cries and beggings, sliding the feather down her hip as she worked the other one in slow circles around her breasts, doing figure eights. She then slid both feathers up the swollen mounds and across the nipples, caressing the hard little buds with soft movements.

She tormented Miranda's breasts with the feathers for long minutes, stimulating them outrageously. Miranda's breasts longed to be squeezed hard, and her nipples longed to be sucked, pinched, and chewed, but all she was getting was the light caress of the feather, which added to her heat but did nothing to satisfy her.

Ellen sat back, her back sore, sliding the twin feathers across Miranda's belly. Miranda gasped and arched her back helplessly as the delicate tendrils of air slipped over her stomach muscles. Then they moved down between her splayed thighs, caressing her inner thighs again.

After a minute, they moved up onto her pussy mound, rubbing, stroking, twirling, dancing, making Miranda hump again and again helplessly.

"Ellen...ahhhh," she moaned.

"Have patience, little one," Ellen smiled.

She twirled one feather up and down the girl's cunt cleft, causing a moan of anguish.

She then halted and removed a small pair of scissors from the bag. She began to snip away at Miranda's cunt hair, cutting it very close to the skin. With just the stubble remaining, she put away the scissors and picked up a small bottle. She poured its contents across Miranda's crotch, then sprayed shaving foam onto it.

Miranda had no idea what was going on, though as she felt the razor move along her lower abdomen, she guessed.

"Ellen!" she gasped. "Don't!"

"Shhh."

"But you can't!" she moaned.

"Yes! I can."

She carefully shaved down Miranda's cunt, then along her inner thighs. There was little if any, hair there since Miranda kept her bush small for the tiny bikinis she liked to wear at the beach in summer. Ellen rubbed the girl's crotch dry and gazed at the results.

Miranda's little cunt crack now stood out bare and bald, not a hair to be seen. She was as smooth as a little girl, and Ellen removed one of her gloves to rub her bare fingers up and down the naked mound.

"Doesn't that feel nice?" she sighed. "Wait until you see how you look, little one."

She moved back to let her friend see and admire how pretty Miranda's bare puffy cunt mound was, exchanging grins with the women. Kristen reached down and stroked Miranda's breast, then squeezed it a few times before rubbing her hand over her puffy cunt mound. Charlotte and then Valerie stroked the naked cunt, each shaking her head in dejection that they could do no more.

They moved back and resumed their seats. Ellen bent over now, bringing her face close to Miranda's bare crack. She began fingering her cleft, stroking her fingers up and down between her pussy lips, prying them wide and massaging each side, then slipping her tongue through and lapping at the glistening pink cunt skin.

"Ohhhhhhh," Miranda moaned.

Ellen began to lick her clitty, sliding her fingers down into her fuck pipe and pumping them in and out. Her talented tongue slithered across Miranda's clit with deft, careful motions, soon bringing the girl to a shattering climax.

Ellen watched the girl's muscles straining as she pulled

helplessly at the ropes, her body jerking and shaking through the powerful climax. The other women looked on hungrily, Kristen and Susanne rubbing at their pussies as they watched.

She went back to work, sucking at the girl's clitty, working her lips and tongue over it, gnawing at it with her teeth, and fucking her fingers into the girl's bubbly hot snatch.

She brought her to another cum, then another, then another, Miranda's howls of pleasure echoing off the bare walls. All three of the spectators were rubbing their pussies now. Kristen and Charlotte had raised their skirts while Valerie had opened her pants and shoved her hand down into them.

Ellen straightened and picked up another of her tools, a narrow, high-speed vibrator. She clicked it on and began rubbing it up and down between Miranda's cunt lips. She pumped it in and out of her fuck tunnel several times, then pressed it directly against her clitty.

Within a minute, as Ellen rubbed the vibrator back and forth across her fuck button and pumped her fingers into her steaming snatch, Miranda came again, shrieking in glorious ecstasy, her limbs straining against the ropes as her head slammed from side to side.

Ellen removed the buzzing vibrator, rubbing her hand up and down Miranda's cunt as the girl whimpered and fell back to earth. She massaged the girl's creamy cunt mount for long seconds, then began licking and sucking at her again.

Her mouth tired, she moved back and, out of pity, motioned an eager Valerie forward. Valerie took her place between the girl's splayed legs, gazing excitedly at her tender, red, puffy cunt entrance. She bent and began licking at her clitty as she pumped a finger up and down inside her.

She soon worked the writhing blonde into another orgasm.

Then it was Kristen's turn. She stuffed her tongue jeep into Miranda's fuck pipe, pushing it up high, mashing her lips and face into the girl's raw fuck pad. She flittered her tongue back and forth inside the narrow tube, her fingers working over Miranda's clitty at the same time.

She soon had Miranda shaking and humping and crying out in agonized pleasure again. The weary, dazed, bedraggled, sweat-coated young blonde had no idea what was happening anymore. All she knew was the tightness in her chest and the rawness of her cunt.

Charlotte took Kristen's place and worked Miranda into two fast orgasms that left her panting and almost unconscious. Then Ellen moved in again. She had removed her G-string and had on a very long, very thick, strap-on dildo.

She knelt between the trembling young woman's legs, rubbing the head of the dildo up and down Miranda's cunt entrance. Miranda had heard of dildos but had never seen one, let alone had one inside her, so when she felt the bloated plastic cock sliding down into her spastic cunt tube, she gasped in both pleasure and shocked amazement.

"E... Ellen?" she moaned, her voice quivering.

"Yes darling," Ellen breathed, settling her upper body down on Miranda's, then thrusting her hips forward. She sent the thick dildo stabbing up into Miranda's cunt with violent energy.

Miranda screamed, straining once again against the bonds. Her mouth opened wide in shock, and she gurgled in wonder.

"Do you like my plastic cock, Miranda?" Ellen purred. "I know how you like to have your little pussy pumped by a cock. So I got one for you."

She lay flat atop the young blonde, her teeth nipping at her earlobes, her hands stroking the hot, swollen young breasts that pushed up against her. She ground her hips in slow circles and jerked them from side to side.

The base of the dildo was a soft rubber pad that cleverly rested right up against Ellen's clitty. The movements of the dildo sent it grinding against the older woman's fuck button, with delicious pleasure the result.

She mashed her lips down on Miranda's gaping mouth, stuffing her tongue halfway down the shaking girl's throat as she began to hump into her. The long, fat plastic cock started to pump in and out of Miranda's fuck tunnel, grinding over her clitty and straining cunt lips as it moved.

"Oh, God!" Miranda cried, "Oh Christ!"

The dildo moved faster inside her, the head punching against her cervix, the thick girth forcing her elastic cunt walls to bloat outwards as it slid up and down.

"Ungh! Unnnngh!" Miranda gasped, moaned, and cried in pure pleasure.

Ellen's body rubbed down hard against Miranda's, flesh stroking flesh. Her breasts mashed against Miranda's, moving up and down, then side to side as she jerked her body around. Her hips jerked and humped and thrust, plunging the dildo with hard, savage strokes.

The three watching women buried their fingers in their snatches as they watched. Each urged Ellen on silently, their eyes ravenous as they watched each hard, deep thrust of the fat plastic cock.

Ellen grunted, her eyes clenching, opening, and closing, her head pulling up and back as she threw her hips hard against Miranda's crotch. She gasped and groaned as the base of the dildo ground furiously against her clitty.

Miranda came first, her scream silent as her chest was locked in a vice-like grip by the incredible power of her climax. Her body pulsed and throbbed as a crackling ball of sexual electricity surrounded her, tearing her apart.

Her head jerked back, slapping again and again into the mattress, her body stiffened, her back arched, and her head pulled back hard, raising her upper body off the bed as she trembled and jerked and gurgled helplessly.

She still could not breathe. Her cum went on and on as Ellen sent the plastic cock pounding up into her with savage thrusts.

Ellen came then as well, her face drawn into a snarl, her eyes closed tightly. She humped furiously against Miranda, her hands coming down beneath the girl and cupping her buttocks, squeezing them hard, her fingers digging into the soft flesh as she sought to ram the dildo even harder into the shuddering girl's fuck box.

Miranda's face was turning red, then white from lack of oxygen. No one noticed. No one cared. Ellen was in the middle of her own gut-churning orgasm and would not halt her furious humping for anything. The three spectators stared with delight at the sight of the fat cock as it pistoned in and out of the girl's bare crack.

Finally, Miranda passed out from lack of air. Ellen continued to fuck her for long, long seconds before collapsing over her with a groan of relief.

8 – Partner Shake Down

Miranda's heart pounded as she quickly leafed through the papers on Ellen's desk. She was terrified the woman would come back suddenly and catch her there. Being her law clerk gave her access to her outer office, not her inner office. Ellen and her secretary were supposed to be at lunch, but she was still anxious.

She checked through her out basket as Alicia had advised, then quickly jerked several contracts and a couple of file folders free, scurrying across the room to the door, then slipping through and out into the outer office. She tucked the papers into her briefcase and left the office, going down the hall to John's office.

He and Alicia glanced through the assortment of contracts, muttering to themselves, then John held up one.

"Now, here's a likely enough prospect," he said. Alicia glanced at it and nodded, then returned to one of the contracts. She studied it and then handed it to Miranda.

"Change the fourth clause here," she said, pointing.

"She's already checked it out, so all you have to do is get on her secretary's word processor quick, change the one to a ten, print it again, then return the new contract to her out basket."

John was typing rapidly at his own word processor while Alicia sorted through the other contracts.

"This one here," she said. "Change 'party of the first part' to 'party of the second part,' and vice versa."

The printer started up, and a paper came sliding out. John

grabbed it and handed it to Alicia, who glanced at it, then at him.

"Isn't this a little much?" she said.

"Why? Somebody will probably catch it."

"If Ellen sees this, she'll settle for a small amount out of court. That little boy could get millions from the chemical company.

"Who cares?"

Alicia scrunched it up and tossed it at him, leafing through the contracts again.

"How about this one?" he said, pointing at another case file. "If we change the age of this girl here to eighteen from sixteen, she'll wind up in adult court and find herself in prison with a bunch of bull dykes like Ellen."

"Try to keep it on your tiny mind, John, that it's Ellen we want to fuck, not some poor kid."

"You seen this bitch? I have. She needs to get fucked."

"Fuck off, John."

"You didn't say that when I had my cock up your pussy," he sneered.

She glared at him. He'd been reminding her of that for two days now. She turned to Miranda and handed her back the contracts.

"Just do what I said," she motioned to the door.

Miranda hurried back to Ellen's office and turned on her secretary's word processor. She called up the correct files, changed a couple of numbers and words, then printed out the new version of the contracts. She hurriedly put them back into Ellen's out basket.

She snuck out again, but for the rest of the afternoon, worried that Ellen would find them and know who'd done the changes. She was anxious and fearful when Ellen called her into her office that afternoon, but the woman wasn't angry.

She took Miranda into her lap and began stroking her hair and fondling her breasts. She slid a hand up Miranda's skirt and began to jerk her off. Miranda ground her ass into Ellen's lap, mewling helplessly as the woman worked her thumb against her clitty and pushed her fingers into her cunt.

She came, jerking and shaking in Ellen's arms.

Ellen pushed her off and down to her knees before the chair. She spread her legs, and Miranda gripped her panties and slid them down and off. She began lapping at her cunt as Ellen sat back and stroked her hair.

* * *

The next day she had to do a slow strip tease first thing in the morning, dancing and wriggling to music while Ellen watched. Then, naked, she knelt between her legs and licked her to two straight orgasms.

Ellen was particularly horny that day, calling her back four times to lick her to climax. Miranda wasn't as bothered by that as she might have been, especially after she saw Alicia coming out of Meyer's office, rubbing her behind.

"Bastard fucked me in the ass," she winced.

Miranda scrunched up her face in sympathy. She'd never been fucked up the ass and never wanted to be.

"We have to get rid of that bitch soon," she said "So I can get Meyer off my back."

"She's real horny today. I've had to eat her five times."

"Next time she calls you, let me know and make sure the door is unlocked."

"Are you, uh, going to catch us?"

"Sort of."

"But I'll get fired."

"No, you won't. We'll claim sexual harassment and threaten to sue. They'll keep you on to avoid the scandal, but Ellen will be fired."

"But she's been kind of nice to me," Miranda protested.

"Nice? That whore? Listen to me, you dumb bitch. She s only playing at being nice for now. Try going against her will on anything and see how nice she is. There used to be a guy called Norman here. Ellen had some guy seduce his wife, then play a sex game with her where she pretended to be a prostitute. The guy turned out to be a cop and arrested her for prostitution, with her own words on tape to convict her."

"Wow."

"Wow, yeah. The woman only got a fine, but Ellen ensured everyone knew about it. It was a major scandal. Norman had to resign, and he and his wife were divorced. She's done a lot worse than that too."

Miranda was called back only an hour later. She dutifully called Alicia and then went to Ellen's office.

"Hello, little baby," Ellen said, sliding her tongue out of her mouth.

"Boy, are you horny again?"

"You bring out the worst in me, sweetling."

"Want me to lick you?"

"Take your clothes off first."

"Uh, do I have to?"

"Yes."

Miranda stripped off quickly, waiting nervously for the door to open. Ellen stood up this time and started taking off her own clothes. She stripped down to her black bra, panties, stockings, and garter belt, then took off the panties. She moved against Miranda and drew her into her arms, kissing her passionately.

Their hands moved over each other, squeezing, stroking, and caressing as their tongues slithered together. Ellen pulled backward and dropped into her couch, laying sideways with one leg up on the back.

"Come to Mama," she leered, patting her crotch.

Miranda crawled onto the couch and bent over her crotch, then began to lick. Her fingers pried at Ellen's cunt lips as her tongue slid up and down between them.

Ellen lay her head back and gripped her head, sighing in bliss. Her body soon began to hump the girl's face as Miranda's by-now-experienced tongue pumped in and out of her fuck tunnel.

The door burst open suddenly, and Meyer and John walked in. They acted astonished as the two women yelped and tried to cover themselves.

"Well, well, well. I might have known." Meyer sneered. "You never would go out with me, Ellen, honey."

"You slug! Get out of my office!" Ellen snarled.

"Nice tits there, Ms. Rogers." John snickered.

"I wonder what Mister Moore will say when he hears about this," Meyer taunted. "Since he was born again, he's become more than a little intolerant about things like this."

Alicia came in then and whistled at Ellen, who turned and glared daggers at her.

"All of you get out!" she shrieked.

"Why don't you come with me, you poor thing?" Alicia oozed at Miranda, helping her put her clothes around herself.

"Isn't she a bit young for you, Ellen?" Meyer glared.

"Abusing the help does not sit well with any of the senior partners, particularly in such a... perverted, sick way."

Alicia led Miranda out, and Meyer motioned John to the door as well.

"You fucking bastard!" Ellen hissed.

"That I am, but at least I'm not fucking little boys."

"She's an adult."

"She's a summer clerk. What did you do? Threaten to fire her if she didn't come across?"

"I did no such thing!"

"I don't think you'll be able to prove that, my dear. I think old Moore will be so nauseated with this performance that he'll boot your pretty little ass out the door." His teeth shone as he smiled broadly.

"So you want me to resign? Right? You fucker!"

"Resign? Perish the thought. Why should I have you resign when I can have you here, voting as I want?"

Her eyes narrowed as he sat back on her desk and grinned malevolently.

"I'm going to make the senior chair soon anyway. I hear old Morgan has heart problems. Hell, maybe we can send you in there like this. That should get him to kick off for good."

"I refuse!"

"If you refuse, there'll be a huge scandal. You'll not only be fired but be the subject of ridicule all across the city, if not the country. I don't think you want that, baby."

"Fascist male slime!"

"It's not all that bad. You'll get to keep the little blonde, and maybe I'll even loan you, Alicia, from time to time."

"Alicia! That ice queen?!"

"You're the ice queen, honey. She's just an ice princess. I'm sure you'll enjoy putting her through the works."

"She'll do that?" Ellen looked at him warily.

"She'll do anything I tell her to do, including suck that pussy of yours. Maybe you can even shave her muff off. I assume you made that cute little blonde bald between the legs."

Ellen shrugged, trying to regain some semblance of dignity once more as she sat naked on the edge of the couch.

"And I'll have to vote for you when your name comes up for acceptance?"

"And after."

"You fuck," she glared.

"That too." He reached down and gripped her arm, hauling her to her feet.

"Hey!"

"I do fuck, and I've had my eye on your cunt for many years."

"You can just forget it!"

"I don't think so. You've clawed your way up this far. You won't give it all up to avoid a cock up that tight cunt of yours."

He whirled her around, shoved her into the side of her desk, and then slammed her belly down on the top. She gasped as her tits were mashed into the desk. She tried to wriggle away, but Meyer shoved down on the center of her back with one hand as he kneed her legs apart and took out his cock.

"Get off me! You fucker!"

"That's what I'm going to be all right!"

She clawed at the desk, trying to pull out from under his hand, but he just pushed down harder. He took his cock out through his zipper and nudged it against her fuck tunnel.

Never in her life had she had a cock inside her, and she cursed wildly as she tried to avoid one now.

But his cockhead easily parted her cunt lips. Her twat, still hot and wet from Miranda's tongue job, was easy prey for his throbbing red cock. He laughed as she cursed him, thrusting himself deep inside her.

"Ahhh," she cried, "Ohhh, G... God!"

"No, just me, cunt," he hissed. He began humping wildly into her cunt, his fingers digging into her neck as he shifted his grip upwards. His free hand slid under her and began to twist and squeeze her tittie as his cock pumped in and out of her body.

"Bet you really like this, whore," he panted. "Fucking dyke slut! Think you're too good for a cock, do you?" He pumped furiously, his cock slicing back and forth between her pussy lips as she moaned and slapped helplessly at the top of the desk.

"Uhhhh!" she groaned.

"Fucking queer, fuck-hole!" he sneered. "Take that cock! Ungh! Ungh! Yeah! Nice and tight! Just like a virgin!"

His hips smashed into her buttocks with cruel blows as he stabbed his cock into her again and again.

"Bet this is better than the rubber you usually use! Ungh! Ungh! Ungh!" he gasped, panting and sweating as he rutted into her.

"Wait for it! I'm gonna cum! Gonna cum!"

"Nooooo!" she wailed. The thought of male sperm jetting into her belly was nauseating, revolting! She tried again to squirm free, but he was too strong and too excited. His cock pounded in and out of her fuck box as he hissed and grunted and then let out a bellow of pleasure.

His cum spewed out and gushed into her fuck pipe, streaming down to her cervix and frothing through it and into her womb. She gnashed her teeth in rage as he laughed in happiness.

Suddenly the door opened, and two men came in, halting in shock. Jack Moore and Paul Crane, the two most senior partners in the firm, stared in astonishment at the sight there before them.

"My God!" Crane gasped. Moore glared at him, then back at the other two.

"Don't use the Lord's name in vain," he said. "As for you two. You're both disgusting. I think I can speak for the entire senior and junior boards when I want you both out of here by the end of the work day."

"I quite agree," Crane glared.

"But... but..." Meyer said.

"But... but..." Ellen said.

"You knew they were going to come in," Miranda gasped, gazing at Alicia. The two were staring in from the outer office, and Alicia's face was gleeful as she watched Ellen and Meyer getting fired. Alicia put her arm around the petite blonde and walked her out of the office and down the hall to her own office.

"But I thought Meyer was helping you."

"He was going to help me all right. He was going to help make me bow-legged. I won't let some pig use me like a dog."

"But I thought... I mean... How did you know Meyer would do that, fuck Ellen, I mean?"

"Are you kidding? A slimeball like him? I knew when he had her at his mercy, he'd want to screw her. Men always want to show you who's boss by fucking you."

"So you planned for that, but how did you get Mister Moore and Mister Crane to come? Are you fucking them too?"

"Shhh," She led her into her office and closed. "No, that was the great part," she laughed. "Moore called me into his office to complain about the length of my skirts. I did some fast thinking and sort of hinted that Meyer and Ellen were less than moral and that they made me dress like this. I even hinted they were, well, bothering me."

"Bothering you? What a laugh!"

"Well, they were bothering me. I just didn't tell Moore how much." She sat in her executive chair and put her legs on the desk. "I hinted that they were trying to molest me and that I was resisting bravely. I didn't even have to agree to have my skirts lowered," she laughed.

"But how will you get to be a partner now?"

"I told Moore that Ellen and Meyer were the only reasons I wasn't already one, that my record was exemplary, and hinted I was considering making a public complaint about it. He said he'd check, and if things were as I said, I'd be a partner within a week."

"But it's all a lie!"

"Not as far as he'll know. My record is exemplary, and as for the rest, well, what he saw in Ellen's office will convince him it's all true."

"You set me up, too, didn't you?" Miranda glared.

"Sure did," Alicia laughed. "You should have seen your face when Meyer walked in. You looked like you were going to faint."

"You bitch!"

"Oh, calm down. Look what you got out of it."

"What?" Miranda fumed.

"For one thing, this job. You never would have been accepted as a law clerk here if we hadn't needed someone cute for this particular task. Resumes from that pukey little college of yours usually go into the garbage. And not only will you serve the next couple of summers here, but I can also guarantee an offer when you graduate.

"Still," Miranda sulked. "It wasn't fair what you did. That bastard John..."

"I'll take care of old John. We can have fun with him this summer, seeing how much he's willing to grovel. As for you..." She brought her feet down to the floor with a thump and stood up, walking across to where Miranda stood against the door.

"From how you acted earlier, what you and Ellen were doing together wasn't totally unpleasant. Am I right?"

"Well, it wasn't that... bad," Miranda conceded, thinking about all the orgasms she'd had in the club that night and the following day.

"I didn't think so," Alicia's hand stroked the side of her face, then slid down onto her breast. "Lady love isn't such a bad thing, after all, now is it?"

"No, not really," Miranda's groin began to hum, and she swallowed as she watched Alicia's fingers unbutton her blouse.

"I'm glad because the other day with you, my fond memories returned, and I think I'd kind of like a second helping of that sweet little body of yours."

She opened Miranda's shirt, then jerked her bra down, freeing her fat tits. She squeezed them up against her face as she began to suck on her nipples.

Miranda began undoing Alicia's shirt, and soon both were

naked, rolling on the couch together, their lips sliding together, breasts rolling and mashing, legs intertwined, crotches grinding, hands stroking, squeezing, and kneading.

Miranda sucked Alicia to a powerful orgasm as the older girl lay sprawled out on the couch, then Alicia began sucking Miranda's cunt, driving her to a climax within minutes. They worked on each other in a hot sixty-nine for long minutes, then slid their cunts together and began to grind their fuck pads against one another until both came again.

Their moans, whimpers, sighs, and cries of pleasure did not penetrate the thick oak door, and the deadbolt on the door ensured they would not be disturbed. Neither one was aware, however, of the tiny hidden camera in the corner of the room or the little microphones scattered around.

In his office, John watched them with a grin as the VCR recorded every loving detail of their sensual sex play. In his mind, he went over a list of all the sex acts the two would do for him, separately and together, and tried to decide which would be first.

THE END

A Story from

Yesteryear's Stories Reflected Today

CARL. U MAXWELL